The Sign of Zorro

"You would murder three innocent men, just to capture me?" Zorro said. He gazed with contempt at Rafael Montero, the governor of Alta California.

Montero's snake eyes glared at him. "I would murder a hundred more to see you in irons."

A smile flickered beneath Zorro's mask. "Three men—three cuts."

Lightning fast, Zorro sliced three quick cuts on Montero's neck. An oily red *Z* appeared, like a tattoo. The stunned governor clapped his hand over the bloody wound.

"A small memento of Mexico," Zorro said, leaping onto the rail of the balcony. "Remember not to pick the scabs."

For orders other than by individual consumers, Pocket Books grants a discount on the purchase of **10 or more** copies of single titles for special markets or premium use. For further details, please write to the Vice-President of Special Markets, Pocket Books, 1633 Broadway, New York, NY 10019-6785, 8th Floor.

For information on how individual consumers can place orders, please write to Mail Order Department, Simon & Schuster Inc., 200 Old Tappan Road, Old Tappan, NJ 07675.

THE MASK OF ZORRO

A NOVELIZATION BY FRANK LAURIA
STORY BY TED ELLIOTT & TERRY ROSSIO
AND RANDALL JAHNSON
SCREENPLAY BY JOHN ESKOW AND
TED ELLIOTT & TERRY ROSSIO

Published by POCKET BOOKS
New York London Toronto Sydney Tokyo Singapore

A MINSTREL PAPERBACK *Original*

A Minstrel Paperback published by
POCKET BOOKS, a division of Simon & Schuster Inc.
1230 Avenue of the Americas, New York, NY 10020

ISBN: 0-671-51967-0

First Minstrel Books printing July 1998

10 9 8 7 6 5 4 3 2

Printed in the U.S.A.

For Gladys George, Eastside High,
Paterson, New Jersey—a great teacher . . .

THE MASK OF ZORRO

1

IT WAS AS DARK AS DEATH.

The two boys hunched close together inside the wagon. The younger boy, Alejandro, had a knife. Carefully, he cut through the black canvas that covered the wagon bed.

The boys could hear loud voices and drums coming closer. "Freedom! Liberty! *Independence!"* the voices chanted. "Freedom! Liberty! *Independence!"*

Alejandro's knife made one eyehole, then a second. He pressed his face against the canvas and peered outside.

There was a blur of sound and movement. Drums pounded along with the chants. Feet stomped. Hands clapped. Above it all rose rough, angry voices shouting orders—the voices of Spanish soldiers.

"Shut your mouths!"

"You—back in line!"

"Get back there! Keep your distance!"

As Alejandro watched the soldiers push people back, his older brother, Joaquin, became impatient.

Joaquin pulled at his brother's arm. "Come on, Alejandro," he whispered. "It's my turn. Let me see."

Alejandro Murieta was only eight, two years younger than his brother, Joaquin, but he knew enough to keep quiet. He moved aside so Joaquin could peer out one peephole.

Both boys stared in amazement. The town square was jammed with people. The crowd was barely held back by soldiers jabbing their bayonets. The soldiers were outnumbered and looked nervous.

The throng filling the sun-baked square was made up of Mexican peasants. They jeered at the Spanish soldiers in their fancy uniforms.

"Down with the Spanish flag!" someone yelled.

With that, a young peasant snatched the ragged flag flying in the wind. Everyone cheered wildly.

"Use it to clean your floors!" an old man shouted.

Another man climbed the pole to attach a Mexican flag. One soldier tried to stop him, but a group of peasants moved in front of the flagpole. The soldier backed away.

The reason for the crowd's anger was at the other end of the square. In the area protected by soldiers, there were three posts. A man was tied to each post. The men were about to die.

It was 1821. After years of bloody fighting, the Mexican people had finally defeated the Spanish rulers and won their independence. With it they had won Alta California, that fabulous strip of land on the western shore of North America. Now Alta California belonged to the victor, General Santa Anna of Mexico.

Rafael Montero, the hated governor of Alta California, had been recalled to Spain. But true to character, he was not finished. As a final act of power, he chose three innocent men and ordered them shot—in front of their families.

The spirit of justice demanded a champion. . . .

Terrified but excited, Alejandro and Joaquin watched the six-man firing squad march into position.

Bright light suddenly flooded the dark wagon bed. "Hey!" a voice roared. "What are you doing, cutting holes in my wagon cover?"

The boys blinked at the tall man lifting up the rear flap. It was Senor Lopez, the town undertaker. Inside his wagon were four freshly made coffins. Three for the condemned prisoners outside and one for a mystery guest.

The undertaker's narrow lips pinched into a scowl. "This is a place of business!" he scolded. "Not for the games of boys!"

Joaquin nodded sheepishly. "I'm sorry, Senor Lopez. We are just waiting for Zorro."

"Not in here, you aren't," Lopez said wearily. "Go home, muchachos."

Relieved that they wouldn't be punished, Alejandro looked at the undertaker. "Do you think he's really going to come, Senor Lopez?"

The pale, thin undertaker squinted at the hopeful little boy. He looked around and put a finger to his lips. "Someone thinks he will," Lopez whispered.

He pulled away a sheet covering the fourth coffin—revealing a black *Z* carved in the wood.

The boys gaped at the coffin. They glanced at each other, then jumped off the wagon.

"Joaquin! Alejandro!"

The undertaker's sharp voice drew them up short. Slowly the two brothers turned around, expecting the worst.

Instead, Senor Lopez nodded at the shiny coffins. "I carved boxes for your mother and father once," he said sadly. "I would hate to carve two more for you."

The little boys shivered as the point sank in.

"Go home," Lopez said gruffly.

Joaquin and Alejandro hurried away. A moment later they were lost in the crowd.

The angry mob was becoming dangerous. They threw anything they could find at the soldiers—fruit, stones, even shoes. Their chanting grew louder.

"Death to Montero! *Death to Montero!*"

The crowd's war cry rose high above the square to the governor's office. Hearing the shouts, Rafael Montero, the Spanish governor, stepped outside onto the balcony and looked down at the crowded square. His darkly handsome face was calm as he watched the peasants shaking their fists at him. They hated him, but he didn't care. Montero considered them animals, like sheep and cattle.

Swak! A few well-aimed tomatoes splattered near him, but Montero didn't bother to duck.

"Their aim is as hopeless as their future," Montero muttered with a smug smile.

But the truth was, the peasants had won and the Spanish rulers were packing their bags. Even now the palace was being stripped of all valuables. They would pay for Montero's return to Spain.

Enraged at the sight of Montero on the balcony, the

crowd surged against the line of soldiers. Although the soldiers were heavily armed, the peasants were ready to explode.

Down in the square, Joaquin tried to keep track of his little brother. Alejandro was always in danger of being kicked or stepped on as they scooted through the noisy mass of legs.

Both boys tried to creep closer to the firing squad, for a better view. They were a few yards away when a man wearing sandals planted his feet in their path.

The boys looked up and froze. Looming over them was the round moon face of Fray Felipe, the town priest. He wasn't smiling.

"Get back to the mission, you little cow chips!" Fray Felipe growled. "This is no place for you."

The boys glanced at each other, then slipped around the priest and darted into the crowd.

Laughing, Alejandro and Joaquin scrambled through the milling mob. They knew Fray Felipe wouldn't punish them. The brawny priest looked like a bear, but he was as gentle as a lamb.

As the boys neared the other side of the plaza, they heard familiar sounds: children's voices, laughter, scattered applause. Alejandro and Joaquin arrived just as a puppet show reached its climax. There were two figures: one was Zorro and the other Rafael Montero.

Both puppets had been made by hand with loving attention to detail. The Zorro figure wore a black silk mask and silver spurs. The Montero puppet was adorned with jewelry and a fancy sword—just like the real governor.

"I am Don Rafael Montero!" a child actor said in a deep voice. "I have many soldiers! All must obey me!"

The child playing Zorro had stage fright. "No, Don Rafael! I will not obey you!" he shouted. Then he slowed down. "Because, uh . . . because you are . . . stupid and . . . dumb!"

Alejandro couldn't stand it. His hero was being played like a dummy. "Wait, wait! That's no good," he cried, pushing through the ring of spectators. "Zorro should say, 'I spit in your face, Montero! Death to the Spanish high boots! Wherever I carve my *Z,* the people know that—' "

His performance was cut short by the thunder of hoofbeats. All the children looked up and saw three horsemen galloping across the town square. The horsemen paid no heed to the people crowding their path—peasant, soldier, or anyone else. They rode directly toward the group of children. Playtime was over.

Dropping the puppets, the frightened kids dived, ran, and crawled out of the way of the slashing hooves, barely escaping. Their puppets weren't so lucky.

The galloping horses crushed the puppets as they tramped through. After they passed, the children ran back to see if anything could be saved. But the horsemen had left nothing except splintered wood and sadness.

The riders—Don Luis, an aristocrat, and his two bodyguards—galloped to the center of the square. Everyone jumped out of the way of their horses.

Don Luis pulled up his horse in front of the governor's palace. He was tall and lean with a neat goatee and a regal manner. With a disgusted frown he dismounted and marched through the rabble, followed by his bodyguards. Head high, he strode into the great hall. His expression remained stony as he took in the frantic activity around him.

The palace was being taken apart piece by piece. Valuable paintings, silverware, furniture, crystal—all were being carted off by the soldiers. Don Luis shook his head and climbed up the stairs.

As he quickly walked along the hall, Don Luis dodged two servants hauling a rolled-up rug. The door to the main office was ajar. Don Luis stepped inside, anxious to see Governor Montero. He had urgent news.

Montero was standing on the balcony. He had seen Don Luis's dramatic arrival and was slightly amused. He calmly studied the angry mob as he waited.

Montero's snake eyes darted to the glass doors as Don Luis came out onto the balcony.

"Don Rafael," Don Luis said breathlessly. "Santa Anna's men are three miles from the town. You have to go, sir—now!"

Montero shrugged. "The Spanish government would like to thank you for your devoted service, Don Luis." He handed the nobleman an official-looking parchment.

"'This land is the property of the Spanish government,'" Don Luis said, reading the document.

"And in two hours it will be the property of the Mexican government unless I turn it over to you," Montero replied. "I know Santa Anna. He will realize that the noblemen will be dutiful taxpayers, and he will respect your claims." He motioned to a stack of similar documents on a table nearby. "The rest of Alta California I've divided equally among the other aristocrats. I trust you will make sure they receive their grants."

Don Luis picked up the documents and quickly flipped through them. He wasn't happy at what he saw, but he knew he had to be diplomatic.

"Uh, well, sir," he said, addressing Montero politely, "the land you have given me is mostly desert, whereas you have favored Don Peralta with the lush farmlands of—"

Montero cut him off. "One day you'll understand that I've favored you above all, Don Luis."

Montero turned back to the milling crowd below. "Yes, yes." He sighed, as if bored. "Just one last duty to perform."

As Montero watched, the leader of the firing squad began barking orders to his men. It was time for the execution.

Montero turned and moved briskly to the railing. "Get the children out of the plaza," he shouted down to the soldiers. "Immediately!" He looked at Don Luis. "Children should never have to see the things we do."

There was a rush of activity as the soldiers began rounding up children. Everybody was yelling—the soldiers, mothers, children—as they were hauled off. Most of the kids were terrified, but some were angry at missing the big show.

Especially Joaquin and Alejandro, who were dragged screeching and kicking in different directions. As his older brother disappeared, Alejandro became scared. He yanked hard to get free, but the man holding him had an iron grip.

Alejandro blinked. The man wasn't a soldier at all. He wore the brown robes of a monk, like Fray Felipe.

The boy started kicking. "No! No!" he yelled. "Someone has to stop the killings!"

"Someone will," the monk whispered.

Alejandro peered at the monk. Suddenly he stiffened. Beneath the monk's rough robe, he could see shiny black boots with silver spurs and the sharp tip of a silver sword. Alejandro's heart began to pound.

Eyes wide, he looked up and saw a black silk mask inside the monk's hood. Just below the mask was a dashing mustache and the flash of a smile.

Alejandro could hardly breathe.

It was him—Zorro!

"But—but you're . . ." Alejandro sputtered.

The masked man put a finger to his lips. "Shh." He smiled, as if assuring Alejandro that everything would be fine. Then he wheeled and vanished into the crowd.

It took Alejandro a long time to find Joaquin. The boy had to dodge soldiers, horses, and angry peasants as he hunted for his brother.

Finally he spotted Joaquin. His brother was tied with a rope to a group of other children. The group was guarded by only one soldier. Alejandro didn't hesitate. He picked up a stone and threw it, neatly popping the guard on the head.

The guard whirled and charged at Alejandro, who took off through the crowd. Alejandro ducked, circled, and ran right back toward his brother. When he reached the captive children, he plowed into Joaquin, then kept going, closely followed by the soldier.

As Alejandro drew the guard away, Joaquin cut the rope with the knife his brother had slipped him. Once free, Joaquin handed the blade to the boy next to him and lost himself in the confusion.

The brothers knew where to meet. For years they'd shared a secret hiding place that overlooked the plaza—and Rafael Montero's terrace. Separately they made their way to the rooftop.

Before Alejandro could tell his brother about the masked man, Governor Montero signaled the firing squad.

The captain drew his sword. *"Preparen!* Ready!"

Click! The firing squad cocked their rifles.

Alejandro searched the crowd for some sign of Zorro, but everyone was still.

The squad leader raised his sword.

"Apunten! Aim!"

Six rifles pointed at the prisoners. The three men stood straight, facing death with honor.

Heart racing, Alejandro watched the captain bring his sword down.

"Fuego! Fire!"

Six fingers squeezed the triggers.

At that moment the stillness exploded. With a sharp crack, a whip snaked around one rifle and yanked it sideways into the others. Like dominoes, all five rifles swept back to point directly at the captain!

"No fuego! Don't fire! No—"

Six shots shattered his frantic cry. The squad leader crumpled to the ground. Above him a cloaked figure floated in the air like a black angel.

Alejandro saw him first. "Zorro!"

The crowd parted as Zorro dropped lightly on his shiny black boots, sword ready.

"El Zorro!" people yelled. "Viva El Zorro!"

With an athletic leap Zorro reached the prisoners. Three quick slashes of his blade and they were free. A few yards away, the men in the execution squad were hurriedly reloading. Some of the soldiers drew their swords and charged.

Moving like the wind, Zorro thrust at his attackers, his blade a blur of gleaming steel. His skillful defense enabled the prisoners to escape into the crowd.

From his balcony, Montero calmly watched Zorro fight off his soldiers. Quick. Deadly. He anticipated every attack.

Don Luis grasped his own sword helplessly. "We should have known Zorro would try to save them."

Montero gave him a triumphant smile. "I was counting on it." He waved his hand as if dismissing a pet dog. "You'd better go now, Don Luis."

Still smiling, Montero reached for a big iron bell on the wall and began to ring it.

Below, the masked rebel's sword hissed like a snake as he held off two soldiers at once. One of the soldiers managed to cut Zorro's arm before he fell. But the wound didn't seem to slow Zorro down.

Clang! Alejandro and Joaquin looked up when they heard the bell. They both knew it was a signal.

They were right. Instantly three riflemen appeared in the tower below the bell and took aim at Zorro.

Joaquin nudged his brother. "Look!"

Alejandro was a step ahead. He spotted a large stone angel at the edge of the roof. He pushed at the heavy statue with all his might. Joaquin added his weight, and the angel ripped free—crashing down on the three soldiers below.

Zorro spun around at the loud noise and saw the

fallen riflemen. Then he spotted the two boys on the roof above. Zorro started to wave when a bullet spat past his ear. A hail of gunfire churned up the dirt around him as the soldiers attacked. Zorro dived, smashed through a nearby door, and raced up the stairs.

The square became quiet. Alejandro and Joaquin peered over the edge of the roof. The soldiers were reloading. Like the soldiers—and everyone else—the boys waited for Zorro to reappear.

A long shadow slipped across the roof. Two black-gloved hands dropped onto the boys' shoulders. The boys whirled, ready to fight.

Standing over them was a tall, black-masked figure. Alejandro and Joaquin blinked. It was Zorro!

"My thanks to you, gentlemen," Zorro said calmly. He removed a medallion from around his neck. It had an odd design—several circles within a larger circle.

Zorro handed the medal to the older boy. Joaquin's eyes and mouth were wide with amazement as he lifted the medal for Alejandro to see.

It was a ceremonial moment. The medal almost seemed to glow. Zorro put one hand on each boy's shoulder, allowing himself a brief second to share their happiness. Then he was moving to the edge of the roof.

"Now, if you'll excuse me," Zorro called, drawing his sword, "I'm missing my own party."

As lightly as a black cat, he dropped onto an overhang, leaped to a canopy, and landed on Montero's balcony. Another swift step and his sword was scratching the governor's throat.

Montero did not flinch from Zorro's blade. He was determined to die proudly.

"You would murder three innocent men, just to capture me?" Zorro said with contempt.

Montero's snake eyes glared at him. "I would murder a hundred more to see you in irons."

A smile flickered beneath Zorro's mask. "Three men—three cuts."

With lightning speed, Zorro sliced three quick cuts on Montero's neck. An oily red *Z* appeared, like a tattoo. The stunned governor clapped his hand over the bloody wound.

"A small memento of Mexico," Zorro said, leaping onto the rail. "Remember not to pick the scabs."

The masked man whistled. Before the sound faded, a huge black stallion bolted out of the shadows. Black cloak spread like wings, Zorro dropped from the railing onto the horse's back.

As the crowd cheered, Zorro charged through a pack of soldiers, scattering them like bowling pins. Then his horse wheeled and galloped up a flight of stairs!

From their perch, Alejandro and Joaquin saw Zorro's stallion race across the roof and leap into space. For a moment horse and rider seemed frozen against the red sky.

An instant later they landed on the church roof. Zorro turned his horse to face the cheering peasants below. He drew his sword and lifted it high in a gesture of victory. His horse, Toronado, reared up proudly, front hooves pawing the air.

The mob roared. Toronado turned, galloped across the roof, and jumped a wide gap to the next building.

In silent awe, Alejandro and Joaquin watched Zorro's horse float from rooftop to rooftop, then fade away into the setting sun.

As if praying, Joaquin fingered the silver medallion that now hung around his neck.

Just below, on the balcony, Montero also watched Zorro's grand exit. Shaking with pain and fury, Montero removed his hand from his wound.

There on his palm was a bloody *Z*.

The mark of Zorro.

2

THE SKY WAS DEEP PURPLE BY THE TIME ZORRO REACHED the waterfall. A rising moon sent gold streaks across the wall of roaring water. Zorro dismounted and moved to the side of the waterfall. Hidden behind the foaming water was a stone ridge.

Holding Toronado's reins, Zorro led him underneath the ridge to a secret cavern behind the waterfall. The enormous cave was lit by torches set in the stone wall.

Wearily Zorro removed Toronado's silver-studded saddle. He felt tired and bruised from the battle.

"God be thanked. The Spanish are leaving," Zorro muttered, rubbing Toronado's neck. "We are getting a bit old for this, my friend."

As if in reply, the black stallion nodded and slowly walked into his stall.

Legs stiff, Zorro moved to the back of the cave. The huge space was his library, workshop, and retreat.

Besides the shelves filled with books, his worktable, and tools, there was also a practice area for sword fighting.

The fencing area had a raised marble floor with an odd design. A circle pattern—exactly like the one on the silver medal he'd given Joaquin—decorated the floor.

As Zorro walked through his stone fortress, he removed his black mask, then his gloves, then his sword. Bit by bit he put away his secret identity. Finally he sat down at a crude wooden table that held a large gold cross and two candles.

Zorro lit the candles and bent his head. He said a brief silent prayer of thanks. It was a ritual he observed after every mission.

He stood and walked to a short stairway carved into the rock. As he climbed the stairs he was no longer Zorro, the fox. He was Diego de la Vega, family man and wealthy rancher.

A hidden door behind the fireplace slid open. Diego calmly stepped through into a large room. The room was simple but elegant. Great windows overlooked the cliffs and the surf crashing far below.

Diego ignored the fabulous view. Instead he headed straight for another room—the nursery. Inside, his daughter, Elena, was fast asleep. A small cluster of flowers was tied to each pole of the crib. Diego inhaled the romania flowers' familiar scent as he neared.

A young woman sat beside the crib watching over the sleeping girl. Diego nodded at Elena's nanny.

"Do you think she's warm enough?" he whispered.

The nanny sighed. Diego fussed over Elena even more than her mother did. "I always put on an extra blanket for you, senor," she assured him.

Diego nodded his thanks, but his attention was on his daughter.

At two, Elena de la Vega had her mother's beauty and her father's temper. Right now, though, she looked like a sleeping angel, Diego thought, stroking her head.

Elena's nanny smiled and went off in search of Diego's wife, Esperanza.

But Esperanza wasn't in the house.

She was sitting in the darkness on a flat rock, watching the moonlit beach for Diego's return. Esperanza drew her shawl closer to ward off the chill. She was always nervous when Diego rode on a mission. She dreaded the hours of waiting, but tonight she had a bad feeling.

To calm her nerves Esperanza stood up and picked a sprig of flowers for Elena's crib. She glanced up and saw a shadow cross the torchlit window of Elena's room.

Esperanza's heart swelled with relief and joy. Diego had returned home. Clutching the flowers, she hurried back to the house.

As she neared Elena's room, Esperanza could hear Diego's voice.

". . . But the good prince was not afraid of the evil king," he whispered to his daughter. "He raced to the bridge, fighting off a hundred guards."

Diego plucked one of the flowers decorating the crib. He waved the flower like a sword. "Then—looking very dashing and handsome in the afternoon sun—he leaped onto the balcony and thrust his enchanted sword under the king's throat. 'You would kill three innocent men,' the prince demanded, 'just to capture me?' "

Esperanza smiled fondly as she watched Diego proudly recount his adventures. The fact that his daughter was asleep made no difference to him.

"And the bad man said—" Diego turned and saw Esperanza standing in the doorway. She looked radiant in the torchlight. Even after years of marriage he was always astonished by her beauty. In her simple dress and yellow scarf she looked like a young bride. But Diego saw something else in her lovely face: fear.

Abruptly he changed his tone. "Uh, the bad man said . . . something very forgettable," Diego finished hastily.

"And the good prince?" Esperanza demanded. "What did he do?"

"He leaped off the balcony onto his faithful steed, Toronado, and raced home to his beautiful wife, Esperanza, never to do anything foolish or dangerous again."

Laughing, Esperanza moved to Diego's side and put her arm around him. It was good to have her husband home. Together they looked down at their daughter. Elena was smiling in her sleep.

"She loves to hear your stories," Esperanza said.

Diego shrugged. "It's only the sound of my voice. One day she'll have no time for my stories."

Esperanza kissed his cheek. "I never tire of them—why should she?"

Hand in hand they walked toward the hall.

"She already has your mischief," Esperanza told him. "Today she broke that little clay horse you made for her."

Diego laughed. Esperanza slipped her arm around his waist, but her hand brushed his wound.

The pain cut off Diego's laugh and he flinched.

"What is it?" Esperanza asked, alarmed.

"It's nothing, merely a scratch."

"Diego, you swore to me. No more nights waiting up, praying you'll come home alive."

The frightened edge in her voice betrayed her deep concern. Diego heard her.

"Esperanza," he said softly, "the Spaniards are going home. We have fought and won." As they climbed the stairway he paused. "Today in the plaza was Zorro's last ride."

Diego took her in his arms. "Now we can grow old together with our five children."

"Five!" She glared at him indignantly.

"Not enough?"

A slow smile crept across Esperanza's ruby mouth. "I love you, Diego."

She reached out for Diego and held him tightly, almost desperately.

For long moments Esperanza remained locked in his loving embrace. Then a cold sensation sliced through the warmth. She opened her eyes, and her heartbeat froze.

Standing at the base of the stairs, his reptile eyes gleaming with hatred, was Rafael Montero. When their eyes met, Montero's stony features softened.

"Doña Esperanza," he greeted her. "You look as beautiful as ever."

"What brings you here, Don Rafael?" Esperanza asked, her voice cold.

Esperanza knew the governor had always been in love with her. At one time he had courted her. But she hated him and everything corrupt he represented. Montero was nothing but a pompous thief.

Diego slowly turned and smiled. "Ah, Don Rafael!

What an honor to have the governor in our home. Won't you stay for supper?"

Montero gave him a murderous look.

"Of course, what am I thinking?" Diego went on. "You have no time to eat. You're fleeing for your life."

Ignoring him, Montero turned to Esperanza. "I have come to apologize."

Both Diego and Esperanza were caught by surprise.

"I am sorry I could not protect this country from the peasants who have overrun it," Montero declared to Esperanza. "I'm sorry I could not make you love me. And I'm sorry I must leave you without a husband."

Montero raised his arm and snapped his fingers. "Arrest him."

Immediately two guards stepped out of the shadows. They moved up the stairs and took Diego by each arm.

"For what crime?" Diego laughed as they pulled him downstairs. "Not seeing you to the boat?"

Furious, Montero grabbed Diego's arm and squeezed hard. Diego's face betrayed nothing. But when Montero released his grip he saw a streak of blood on Diego's sleeve.

"Blood never lies—Zorro," he said triumphantly. He gestured to the guards. "Take him away!"

The guards dragged Diego to the door.

Esperanza ran down the stairs. "Let go of him!"

Montero tried to block her. "He is a traitor to his country and his class, Esperanza."

Pushing past him, she hurried to Diego's side.

"He is not worthy of you," Montero implored, trying to pull her back.

The moment Montero grabbed Esperanza's arm, Diego exploded. "Don't touch her!" he roared, pitching the guards off him. In the same swift move he relieved one of his sword and spun around to face Montero.

Montero barely got his own sword up in time to deflect Diego's slashing blade. Montero hacked wildly with his own sword, trying to ward off Diego. To avoid their blades, Esperanza hurried up the stairs.

The guards aimed their rifles at Diego but couldn't find a clear shot. Diego and Montero continued to feint and jab at each other as Esperanza looked down in despair.

Quick as a cat, Diego jabbed, slapping the sword from Montero's fist. Then, pressing his blade into Montero's heaving chest, Diego hesitated. To kill an unarmed man, in his home, his wife watching . . .

Whang! A soldier fired point-blank. The bullet cracked past Diego's ear. Instinctively he ducked away.

Montero jumped to his feet, arms raised. "No!" he barked. "This is between us!"

Diego allowed him to pick up his sword. Blades flashing in the torchlight, the two men circled each other. Montero lunged and slashed Diego's chest—a deep cut.

Esperanza gasped when she saw the red stain on Diego's shirt. Montero lunged again, blade slicing at the bright red mark. But Diego wasn't there.

Montero's errant stroke dislodged a torch. As the burning torch toppled to the floor, it set the curtains on fire. Neither of the men noticed as they continued to duel for their lives.

The flames sent long shadows dancing across the wall as Montero backed away from Diego's deadly sword. Suddenly Montero charged. With lightning speed Diego smacked the blade from Montero's hand and pinned him against the wall. Again Montero was at his mercy, cold steel at his throat.

This time Diego knew what he had to do. Blade digging into Montero's neck, he savored the moment.

Clack! The soldiers cocked their rifles.

Diego turned to smile at them. "You heard what he said. This is between us."

"All of us!" Montero cried.

Heart pounding, Esperanza saw a soldier circle behind Diego. She tried to warn him, but the words wouldn't come. In horror she rushed down the stairs.

The soldier—a heavyset lieutenant—fired!

The boom filled the house. Then it was as quiet as a tomb. Instinctively Diego checked to see if he'd been hit.

A small moan cut the silence.

Diego's blood turned to ice. He glanced back. Esperanza clutched her chest and tried to speak. Very slowly she crumpled to the stairs.

Both Diego and Montero turned. The heavyset lieutenant blinked at them, the rifle smoking in his hand.

Numb with shock and disbelief, Diego knelt beside his wife.

Montero stared, eyes strangely blank. An instant later he snatched up his fallen sword and struck, piercing the lieutenant's heart. The heavyset soldier was dead before he hit the floor.

Crazed with remorse, Montero stumbled back to where Diego cradled his dead wife in his arms. "I would never have let any harm come to her," he rasped.

Diego glared at him with cold fury. "She was never yours to protect."

The remaining guard's excited muttering drew Montero's attention. He turned and saw that the burning curtains had become a wall of fire. The mounting flames had reached the ceiling.

Ignoring the raging blaze, Diego gazed down at Esperanza and gently rocked her in his arms.

A child's faint cry roused Diego from his grief.

Elena. The child was alone in her room.

His mind suddenly clear, Diego gently lowered Esperanza's body and sprang to his feet. Eyes stinging and lungs choked with smoke, he moved toward the raging flames to get his daughter.

Without warning, Montero rose up behind him and smashed his pistol down on Diego's skull.

Diego's senses shattered like glass, and he pitched headlong into a yawning blackness.

The remaining soldier drew his sword, intending to stab Diego in the back. Montero blocked him.

"No!" he barked. "Let him live."

Pushing the soldier away, Montero knelt beside Diego, his face twisted. "I want you to live with the knowledge that everything you hold dear is lost," he whispered intensely. "I want you to suffer as I have suffered, seeing you married to the woman I loved."

Diego tried to lift his head. Then he passed out again.

Montero moved to Esperanza's body. Gently he closed her eyes. Behind him the soldier was attending to Diego.

A faint cry roused Montero. He stood up and moved toward Elena's room.

Pain prodded Diego awake.

His eyes half opened, and he tried to turn his head. The slightest move was agony. Stiffly Diego pushed against the hurt and lifted his body.

Bright yellow flames glowed against the darkness. In the dancing firelight Diego noticed a gleaming pool of blood on the floor. It was dripping from his face. Diego tried to wipe away the blood, then stopped.

Both of his hands were chained.

Still groggy, Diego looked around. Slowly he realized he was in some sort of cage. As his vision focused, Diego saw his house engulfed in fire—a living nightmare through the bars of his small cage.

"Elena!" he cried, hurling himself against the steel bars. The cage, which was on a wagon, began to rock. Crazed with pain and horror, Diego continued to shout. "Elena! Elena!"

Orange flames shot high into the sky as the house began to collapse. A whirling fountain of sparks sprayed the darkness. Furiously Diego shook the steel bars, howling like an animal as the blazing roof caved in with a booming crash.

Suddenly a dark figure emerged from the fiery ruins—someone cloaked in a smoldering carpet. The figure pulled the carpet away. It was Montero, and he had something cradled in his arms.

Diego watched Montero swagger toward the wagon, showing him what he'd rescued from the flames.

Elena.

His beautiful Elena was alive. Emotions swinging from anguish to amazement to joy, Diego stretched out his hands, desperate to hold his daughter, to comfort her.

Montero stopped and stood just beyond his reach.

Diego could hear Elena whimpering. "Rafael!" he pleaded hoarsely. "Let me hold her! Give me my child!"

Ignoring him, Montero stroked the baby's cheek.

"There, there." He smiled down at her. "You have your mother's eyes," he murmured.

Montero's mocking voice cut like a razor. Eyes blank with disbelief, Diego stared as Montero turned his back and walked away from the wagon—holding his baby girl.

Diego gathered what remained of his power. "I swear before God, Montero," he shouted, his voice raw and hoarse, "if you do not kill me now, you will never be rid of me!"

Montero didn't even glance back. His laughter trailed after him as he strode away, leaving Diego with his searing grief.

A flash of lightning split the darkness like a fiery sword. The thunderclap unleashed a torrent of rain. As the rain drummed down on the tiny cage, a soldier leaned closer to the bars. "No man survives the dungeon at Talamantes," he jeered.

Diego didn't seem to hear. He slumped against the bars, a broken figure. The soldier gave the bars a parting whack. "Take him away."

The driver lashed his horse, and the wagon started with a jerk. As it began its long journey to Talamantes Prison, Diego de la Vega stared blankly at the smoldering ruins of his life. Then he curled up into a ball, defeated.

High above him the ragged black clouds parted to reveal a huge full moon.

3

Twenty Years Later

THE WATERING STATION WASN'T MUCH.

There was a rickety supply shack for grain, fruit and vegetables, and bullets. The station also had feed bins and a water trough for horses. It was definitely too small for the five soldiers hanging about like buzzards, snatching up the best pieces of fruit.

Obviously they had no intention of paying, the owner observed bitterly. They were like common thieves. He looked back at the wagon. One soldier sat on top, lazily guarding a dusty strongbox.

Trying to control his anger, the owner studied the wanted poster Corporal Garcia had just nailed to his shack. In bold letters the poster read: Wanted: The Notorious Murieta Brothers. Beneath were crude drawings of Alejandro and Joaquin.

A little boy wandered out of the shack. Dark and thin, with lost eyes, he stared up at the wanted poster with a mixture of awe and fear.

The owner shook his head. He had informally adopted the boy a few days earlier. The boy had come to the watering station after his family had been kidnapped. Five people—father, mother, brother, two sisters—had vanished without a trace.

Sergeant Garcia, the soldiers' leader, offered the little boy a peach. Locked in his own world, the boy did not respond.

Garcia shrugged and bit into the peach. The juice ran down his double chin.

Straining to control himself, the owner stepped closer. "Is this how our army is trained?" he demanded. "To steal food and sit around drooling?"

Garcia snorted. "You should be honored to have an officer of my rank steal your fruit."

The pudgy sergeant reached into the wooden bin, searching for another ripe piece of fruit. The owner could stand it no longer. He grabbed the fruit from Garcia's hand and threw it out into the desert.

Enraged, Garcia stood and smacked the owner with a vicious backhand that sent him reeling. The little boy cowered in terror.

But the owner was beyond fear. Sprawled on the ground, he glared up at Garcia with pure contempt. "Look at you," he rasped. "You're supposed to protect us. You're Mexicans, after all!"

He slowly got up and spit at Garcia's feet. "It's worse now than it was under the Spanish. At least then we had Zorro to fight for us."

Garcia rolled his eyes. "Zorro! Only an old cockroach like you would remember him. Good thing he ran away. He would be no match for me."

For the first time, the little boy showed signs of life. His eyes shone as he looked up at the owner.

"Who's Zorro?" he asked solemnly.

Joaquin Murieta idly examined the silver medallion hanging around his neck. From the day Zorro had given it to him, Joaquin had been fascinated by the odd symbol carved into its face—circles within a circle. He often wondered if it had a special meaning. Someday he would ask Zorro, Joaquin told himself. But he'd been saying that for twenty years. Zorro was an old man by now.

Sadly, Joaquin examined the other object around his neck. A rope.

Tied by his neck at the other end was his younger brother, Alejandro. Both brothers were on foot, their hands bound, trailing an armed man on horseback called Jack. Jack had only three fingers on his left hand. The other two jutted from his hatband like grisly feathers.

Despite the situation, Alejandro seemed calm, almost cheerful. His shaggy beard gave his lean, handsome features the look of an artist, but his art was banditry.

The trio crested a hill. Below them was the watering station.

Jack grinned and uncapped his canteen. He took a deep swig, then began pouring water over his dusty, sweaty body. As he took his shower, Jack began to sing in a raspy, cracked voice to the tune of "Camptown Races":

Caught me some bandits plain to see,
Doo-dah! doo-dah!
They're plenty mean, but they don't scare Three

Da-dee-doo-dah-dayyy.
Stayed right on their track,
Climbed right up their back,
So pay the bounty now to me 'cause . . .

Jack paused and cupped his hand to one ear, waiting for Joaquin and Alejandro to finish the verse.

The brothers looked at each other grimly. When they saw Jack was finally offering them some water in exchange for their singing they reluctantly chimed in:

Nobody's as tough as Jack
Yeh!
Nobody's as tough as Jack.

"Now you're gettin' her," Jack congratulated them. "See? Like I done told ya, singin' can lighten yer terrible load. Am I right about that, fellas?"

Jack tossed the canteen to Joaquin, who caught it with both hands. He passed it to Alejandro, whose lips were parched and blistered. Greedily Alejandro lifted the canteen to his mouth. Empty.

Glowering at Jack, he turned the canteen upside down. A single drop fell to the hot sand. Disgusted, Alejandro flung the canteen at Jack's head.

Jack grinned. "Come one, come all!" he hooted. "For the fright of your life! See the notorious Murieta brothers! Horse thieves! Robbers! Plunderers!"

Whooping and laughing, Three-Fingered Jack yanked the rope. Alejandro and Joaquin traded an unhappy glance. Wearily they trudged after their captor.

* * *

The soldiers lounging around the watering station perked up when they saw the three-man parade drawing near. The man on horseback had the air of a bounty hunter. The two prisoners trailing him looked strangely familiar.

Finally one of the soldiers glanced from the wanted poster to the prisoners, then back at the poster. He ripped the poster from the wall and showed it to Sergeant Garcia. "Look! The Murieta brothers! Big as life!"

Annoyed, Garcia squinted at the poster. The other soldiers crowded around to get a look.

Jack slowly got off his horse. He nodded at the poster and reached out his left hand. "You mind?"

A soldier handed him the poster. There was a brief silence as Jack studied it.

Garcia smelled money. He puffed up his chest and moved closer to Jack. "These men are now in the custody of Sergeant Armando Garcia," he announced. "We'll take them the rest of the way. You can claim your bounty in Taxco."

"Yeah," Jack snorted, "when bears start wearin' dresses."

"So how much are we worth?" Alejandro called cheerfully.

Jack frowned. He looked worried, as if he was afraid to hurt the brothers' delicate feelings.

"All figured"—Three-Fingered Jack touched his hat brim in apology—"two hundred pesos."

Alejandro's jaw dropped in disbelief. He looked at Joaquin, who also seemed stunned by the low reward.

"That's it?" Joaquin asked indignantly. "A lousy two hundred pesos apiece?"

Garcia stepped between them. "We're wasting time."

Jack ignored him. He looked at Joaquin and shook his head, wincing painfully. "Uh . . . that's for both," he corrected. "Two hundred pesos, y'know, for the pair."

"What?" Alejandro yelled. "That's crazy! After all the payrolls we've stolen? Don't take it, Jack! You can get more for us!"

"Will you shut up!" Garcia shouted, lashing a hard slap across Alejandro's face.

Instantly a pistol leaped into Joaquin's hand and was pressed against Garcia's skull.

"Touch my brother again and I'll kill you."

Garcia blinked. "I thought you were roped up!"

Joaquin smiled as if the answer was obvious. "That's because you're stupid."

Realizing the whole bounty hunter act was a carefully planned ruse, the soldiers charged at them.

The brothers were ready. In one swift move they stepped aside and dropped to their knees. The rope between them went tight. Alejandro grabbed the rope to protect his neck. Joaquin forgot.

He was choked and dragged when the soldiers tripped over the rope. Alejandro slipped out of his noose and jumped two downed soldiers. A third soldier aimed his rifle at Alejandro's back.

With lightning speed Joaquin snatched a rusty sword from Jack's bedroll and dived. As the soldier fired, Joaquin's blade smacked the rifle aside.

The soldier whirled. With an expert slash of his bayonet, he sent Joaquin's sword flying. Joaquin grinned. He faked left, ducked, and yanked the soldier's rifle out of his hands. Then he swung right and cracked the soldier's head with the rifle butt.

A moment later it was over. The soldiers lay spread-eagled on the ground, and Garcia was still staring down Jack's gun barrel.

It was all the owner could do to keep from applauding. He hastily filled a basket with food and offered it to Joaquin. "With my compliments," he said gratefully.

Joaquin smiled and nodded. The owner beckoned to him. Curious, Joaquin stepped closer.

"They've got a strongbox on their wagon," the owner whispered.

Joaquin nodded. "We know," he whispered solemnly. "That's why we came."

"Ahhh." The owner's face brightened as he finally understood.

Keeping their pistols trained on the soldiers, the brothers collected the rest of the weapons.

As they turned to go, Jack picked up the fallen wanted poster. He studied it, shaking his head. "You know what chafes me about this poster?" he asked sadly. "More than the two hundred pesos—it don't even mention me." He looked to the owner for support. "Ain't I the one figgered how to kidnap the mayor out of his own outhouse?"

Without waiting for an answer, Jack suddenly grabbed Garcia by his shirt. "I'm the guts of this gang!" he screamed. "Without me the whole opera falls apart!"

Sweating, Garcia nodded vigorously.

His rage abruptly spent, Jack went to work. When he

was finished securing his prisoners, Jack hopped onto the soldiers' wagon. Alejandro and Joaquin followed. From the driver's seat Joaquin gave the owner a brief nod of thanks. Then he flicked the reins and the horses started to trot.

As they rumbled away, Jack raised his left hand and wiggled his three remaining fingers. "Remember—Three-Fingered Jack. Armed and dangerous! *Comprende?"*

Garcia and his men couldn't wave back.

All six soldiers were tied up in a tight circle around a large prickly cactus. If anyone shifted even slightly, the whole group would be stung by sharp cactus spines.

Joaquin, Alejandro, and Jack were still laughing long after they'd left the watering station. Finally Joaquin turned to Alejandro and jerked his head at the strongbox. It was time to count the loot.

While Joaquin kept the horses moving at a good pace, Alejandro tried to smash the box's rusty lock with a rifle butt. It stayed locked.

Impatient, Alejandro turned the rifle around and fired. The blast blew the lock to smithereens. The strongbox's lid sagged open on one hinge. Alejandro bent down to scoop out the cash.

Empty! Except for a rat that skittered out over his groping arm. For a moment Alejandro blinked in disbelief. Then it dawned on him: They had been set up.

"Joaquin, stop!" he yelled over the noise of the horses. But Joaquin didn't hear.

Alejandro nimbly leaped from the back of the jouncing wagon into the driver's seat and snatched the reins from his brother.

The horses pulled up short above a steep ravine, raising a cloud of dust. As the dust slowly cleared, the brothers saw six mounted soldiers arrayed across the road ahead.

Frantically the three outlaws spun around. More soldiers had moved up behind them. They were trapped.

Without a word or gesture between them, the Murieta brothers and Jack leaped out of the wagon and tumbled down the ravine.

The soldiers did not move. Their weapons remained in their holsters.

Below them the three outlaws rolled wildly out of control, kicking up dirt trails as they plunged down the steep, bottomless drop.

The brothers landed first, coming to a halt on top of each other. Jack was still sliding and clawing. He careened off a steep ridge into midair.

Bam! The bullet hit Jack before he hit the ground. He howled as he bounced, rolled, and came to a rough stop against something solid. He opened his eyes and looked up at the front legs of a magnificent buckskin horse.

Jack twisted in agony and found himself staring into a smoking pistol barrel. The man holding the gun sat tall on his horse. His posture was perfect, and his eyes burned with intensity. His choice of weapons—a short sword and a saber hanging from his saddle, and a rifle across his lap—marked him as a veteran soldier and a dangerous man.

His name was Captain Harrison Love, and his mission was to kill the Murieta brothers.

Behind him were ten mounted soldiers carrying lances. As Jack gaped in fear, Love holstered his pistol and lifted the rifle to his shoulder.

Jack turned and saw he was aiming at Alejandro and Joaquin, who had scrambled to their feet and were running for the dense brush.

Bam! Joaquin's leg collapsed under him, and he fell heavily. A few yards ahead, Alejandro stopped and raced back to his wounded brother.

The mounted soldiers advanced as Alejandro desperately tried to drag Joaquin up a short bank into the underbrush. There was no chance they'd make it.

"Get going!" Joaquin ordered. "Go!"

Alejandro didn't seem to hear. Ignoring the oncoming soldiers, he continued dragging his brother toward cover. Joaquin drew a small pistol from his sleeve and shoved it under Alejandro's chin.

"I said, go!"

It wasn't the gun but the pleading look in Joaquin's eyes that convinced Alejandro. By remaining free he'd be able to rescue Joaquin. As the charging horsemen thundered closer, Alejandro spun around and sprinted for the brush above the bank.

The horsemen surrounded Joaquin, their sharp lances pointed straight at him. There was a momentary silence as Joaquin stared at them defiantly. Then the circle of horses opened to allow Captain Love to pass.

Love's buckskin horse slowly trotted to Joaquin's side and stopped. Love held a saber in his hand.

"I want you to know I consider this an honor," Love

said, his voice as cold as the grave. He nodded at a nearby soldier. "Prop him up."

The soldier dismounted and forced Joaquin to sit up, despite the pain in his wounded leg.

Love drew back his saber.

Before he could strike, Joaquin moved. He spit in the soldier's face and at the same time drew the small pistol from his sleeve and aimed it at himself.

Crack! Joaquin fell back dead, proudly denying Love the "honor" he craved.

The horses reared back, and their riders gasped fearfully, stunned by Joaquin's act. All except Captain Love. Face blank, he lifted his saber. With one powerful stroke he severed Joaquin's head. Joaquin's medallion sailed free and landed on the dry ground, its face stained shiny red.

Shock hit Alejandro like a club. Hidden in the thick brush, he watched in raging horror, unable to utter a sound. With all his soul Alejandro swore revenge on Love and all like him.

Slowly Captain Love drew a silk handkerchief from his sleeve and carefully wiped his blade. His ice blue eyes scanned the dense brush above the ravine.

"Go find the brother—now!" he ordered.

One soldier held back as the rest galloped off to hunt down Alejandro.

"What do you want us to do with this one, sir?" he asked, pointing at Joaquin's body.

Love turned his buckskin horse.

"Bury the body. Bag the head."

After hours of intense searching, the soldiers realized they'd never find Alejandro. From the top of the ravine all they could see was an endless expanse of thick trees with dense branches, and darkness was falling.

Reluctantly, Captain Love led his men out of the ravine. Slung over one of their horses was Three-Fingered Jack, alive and trussed up like a roped calf.

Alejandro remained hidden long after they had left. Finally, when the moon was high, he carefully approached the site of Joaquin's death.

Alejandro's face was ghostly pale in the moonlight, and his sunken eyes were shadowed by exhaustion. Blood marked the spot where his brother had died. As Alejandro knelt down beside the spot, a glint of light caught his attention.

The moonlight was reflecting off a bright metal object between the stones. Hesitantly, Alejandro reached down. It was Zorro's silver medallion, still stained with Joaquin's blood. Alejandro stared at it for a long time, then clutched it tight in his fist, tears streaming.

Alone in the cold, silent darkness, he lay hunched beside his brother's grave, his body racked with grief.

The moonlight rippled over the calm waters of a secluded cove. Farther out at sea could be seen the bobbing lights of an anchored sailing ship.

A torch flickered at the mouth of the bay.

Minutes later the dark lines of a longboat cut across the shimmering water and approached the shore.

A lone rider came out of the shadows and trotted slowly to the water's edge. Trailing behind his buckskin horse was a tall gray stallion with an empty saddle.

A bloodstained cotton sack hung from Captain Love's saddle. Inside it was Joaquin's head.

Love watched the longboat draw near. Two sailors

leaped out of the boat and waded ashore, tugging the boat onto the beach.

A dark, hooded figure jumped out and approached Captain Love. Love saluted and handed him the reins of the waiting horse.

The hooded figure mounted the gray stallion, and the two men galloped off across the dark sand.

4

TALAMANTES PRISON WAS A FOUL, SUNLESS TOMB.

No one had ever escaped, and no one had ever lived to finish his sentence. Within the dark, moldy walls one could hear the screams of lost souls.

Two horsemen rode into view and pulled up to a long hitching post. Love and his hooded companion tied their mounts with the other horses. Then the hooded figure motioned for Love to wait and marched inside, alone.

The room was in darkness when the hooded figure entered. His torch spilled light over the walruslike body of the warden, snoring on a bed in the corner.

The hooded figure quickly crossed the room, picked up a washbasin full of filthy water, and hurled it into the sleeping man's face.

Gasping and blubbering, the warden reared up, flailing his arms. "Get away from me—get away! Don't touch me!"

Coming out of his nightmare, he blinked at the hooded figure standing over him. "What do you want?" he croaked, his voice quavering with fear. "Who are you?"

The figure pulled back his hood. Eyes bulging, the warden stared at the darkly handsome older man with silver-tipped hair.

"Don R-Rafael?" the warden stammered. He scrambled out of bed and tried to pull himself together. "Don Rafael, sir, I thought you were . . ." He caught himself and managed a weak smile. "What are you doing here?"

When Rafael Montero replied, the warden knew his mission would be difficult.

Finding a prisoner after twenty years in the deep tunnels was like trying to find a lost grain of sand in the desert. The warden led the way, torch held in front of him. Montero was right behind him, followed by a guard named Ordaz, carrying another torch.

They moved slowly down the dank passage. The cellblocks were all wet stone and rusted iron bars. The prisoners lay huddled inside like piles of rags.

Impatient, Montero moved closer to the warden. "His name is Diego de la Vega," Montero reminded him sharply. "I know he was brought here."

The warden's torch sent long shadows dancing across the walls as he checked each cell.

"De la Vega . . ." the warden repeated. "Twenty years ago? Probably a box of dust by now. Not that we give them coffins." The warden giggled. "You can't believe how fast they die around here."

"Not this one," Montero said with a tight, bitter

smile. "This one would make a special point of dying slowly."

The warden led them down a winding stone staircase to a basement cellblock. The damp, rat-infested dungeons made the upper cells seem luxurious. What little air filtered down was stale and tainted.

Montero glared at the warden, who was standing at the rusted iron door to the cellblock.

"Open it," Montero snapped.

The rusty hinges creaked when the warden unlocked the door. Montero stepped inside the foul-smelling hall and began walking past the cold, wet cells.

"Diego de la Vega . . ." the warden murmured. "Don't remember names much. After a couple of years we call 'em what we want, anyway."

"He had another name," Montero said smugly, "remembered only by the peasants. They thought him invincible." He snorted as if at some silly, long-forgotten fable.

"You don't mean Zorro?"

The warden's voice was too loud in the small space, and the name echoed down the cellblock.

Montero stared at him with hatred. "Yes," he said quietly, "Zorro."

At Montero's insistence the warden and his guard, Ordaz, hauled the prisoners out of their cells and lined them up for inspection. As extra security, the warden had guards posted along the block, clubs ready.

"Doubt you'll find the likes of him in this bunch of rabble."

Montero stared at the wrecked shells of humanity shuffling into place. Then he took the warden's torch and began walking slowly along the line of doomed men. The flickering torchlight illuminated their sunken, haggard faces, one after another. Montero passed the bowed gray head of an old man, walked on, then stopped.

Moving back, Montero lifted the old man's chin and squinted closely at his face. Everything about the old man was gray: his long, matted hair, grizzled beard, pale skin, empty eyes.

Montero stepped away, not realizing that the old man was indeed Diego de la Vega. Twenty years in the sunless, airless pit had turned him into a ragged animal.

Montero was still trying to decide—could this be Diego?—when the warden spoke up.

"If anyone among you was once the man known as Zorro, please show yourself. If there is anything left of you to show."

A quavering voice called out from the shadows. "I'm Zorro!"

Startled, Montero left the old man and moved in the direction of the voice. He lifted his torch. The face was that of a bony old geezer. The geezer made a pathetic show of sword-fighting in the air.

"They took my mask, my sword, my horse," he squealed.

"Shut up, you stinking old troll!"

Montero turned and saw a huge black man grinning at him.

"I am Zorro," the black man growled. "I'm the man you want."

"Lies, more lies!" someone shouted. Montero lifted his torch and saw a diseased, pitted face. "Anyone can see you're too tall. I'm the one. Take me!" the man jabbered.

"No, I'm Zorro!"

"Zorro here!"

"I'm the great Zorro!"

Suddenly all the prisoners were calling Zorro's name. The sound echoed wildly inside Montero's brain. He began backing away from the horrible faces, driven out of the cellblock by the power of Zorro's name.

Montero half ran to the stairway. When he emerged from the prison, Love was waiting with the horses.

"Did you find him?" Love asked.

Still shaken, Montero glared angrily. "Let's get back to the boat."

Watching Montero's hasty flight, Ordaz, the chief guard, shook his head. Just like all the big shots, Ordaz thought. They come in, stir up trouble, and let somebody else clean up their mess.

Ordaz turned to his men. "Lock 'em up!"

The guards roughly shoved the prisoners back into their cells, secured their leg cuffs, and locked the doors. Despite their brutality, the prisoners kept shouting, "Zorro! Zorro!" at the top of their lungs.

Diego was the only man not shouting. But his heart was racing with long-forgotten excitement. He felt his moment had finally come, even when he was thrown roughly to the floor and locked into his leg chains.

In the next cell Ordaz gave the last prisoner a vicious shove. It was the ancient geezer who had first claimed to be Zorro. The old man crashed against the wall and fell like a sack of bones—dead.

Ordaz took one look at the man's wide, lifeless eyes

and called a passing guard. "Get him out of here before he starts to stink!"

The guard grabbed the old man's legs and dragged his body along the stone corridor. Ordaz watched them leave, then paused for a final look around, his back to Diego's cell.

It was a mistake.

With ghostly quickness Diego whipped the rope belt from his pants and looped it around Ordaz's throat. The guard tried to summon help, but nothing came out. Diego yanked hard, and the guard's skull clanged against the iron bars.

Ordaz slumped to the floor.

Diego grabbed the guard's key ring, unlocked the door, and dragged him inside. Smiling, Diego picked another key to unlock his leg chain. It didn't work.

Diego's smile became a frantic grimace as he tried all the keys on the ring. None of the keys fit. Crushed, he dropped the key ring and tried to think.

Diego searched Ordaz for something he could use to free himself. He found a dagger in Ordaz's boot. First he tried to spring the leg lock with the knifepoint—nothing. Then he tried to dig the ring out of the wall—useless.

Defeated, Diego bowed his head. His eye fell on something dangling from Ordaz's belt: his powder horn. Hands trembling, Diego poured some black gunpowder into the leg cuff's keyhole. He tore off a strip of Ordaz's shirt to wad the powder. Then he wrapped the rest of the shirt around his foot for protection.

A pouch on Ordaz's belt held shot and flint. Diego struck a flint against the dagger. The powder wad stuffed in the keyhole began to smolder. Diego blew the tiny spark to life. The crude fuse burned quickly.

To shield himself Diego hauled Ordaz's body between him and the burning homemade bomb.

Phwoom! The blast blew the lock apart, searing Diego's leg like a barbecued chicken. He tore the flaming rag from his foot, teeth clenched. He screamed silently as he pulled the cloth from his bloody flesh. Thankful that he still had all his toes, he wiggled them to make sure they still worked.

Ordaz had not been so lucky. A large chunk of metal jutted from his chest. Diego shoved him aside without remorse. He stood up, wincing as raw pain stabbed his mangled foot.

Diego glanced down at Ordaz's feet, checking the dead guard's boots. They were about his size.

After dinner two guards returned on burial detail. One carried an empty canvas sack over his shoulder. Diego heard approaching footsteps and staggered into the cell where the old man lay dead.

Panting from the effort, he slowly pulled the old man's corpse to the door.

Far down the hall the guards unlocked the door to the cellblock. In no particular hurry they strolled down the row of cells. Dead men always waited.

When they came to the old geezer's cell, the guards worked quickly. They stuffed his corpse into the canvas sack and hauled him away.

As the guards shuffled past Diego's cell they didn't notice that it was now occupied by two dead bodies: the ancient geezer and a barefoot Ordaz.

Just outside the high stone walls of Talamantes Prison was the cemetery. Rows of crooked crosses glowed like trapped ghosts in the moonlight. By the time the guards reached the graveyard they were puffing. They carried the sack to a freshly dug grave and dumped it into the shallow hole.

Sweaty with effort, the two men quickly shoveled dirt over the sack. They paused to breathe the cool night air for a few minutes. Then they wearily trudged back to the prison.

As their footsteps faded, silence fell like snow over the graveyard.

A strange chewing sound broke the quiet.

The fresh mound of dirt shifted in the moonlight. Suddenly it caved in like a broken egg. A bony hand clutching a knife clawed through the earth—and reached up for the sky.

Gasping for breath, Diego stabbed and slashed at the dirt-covered sack. But as he cut through, falling earth filled his mouth and nose. Choking, sputtering, and heaving, he fought desperately to rip away his burial shroud.

Suddenly Diego sat bolt upright in his grave. Dirt streaming off his body, he wheezed and coughed, struggling wildly to breathe fresh air. Finally he slumped back, trying to gather his strength. He sat there for a moment, like a specter taking a moonbath, and then a slow smile crept across his ghostly face.

A smile that would have horrified the Grim Reaper himself.

Pushing himself up, Diego tried to stand. Even wearing Ordaz's boots, his injured leg buckled under the intense pain. Diego took a deep breath and looked around. He yanked a nearby cross out of the ground and propped it under his arm.

Using the wooden cross as a crutch, Diego hobbled toward the horses tied to the hitching post at the edge of the graveyard.

5

THE COVE WHERE RAFAEL MONTERO'S SHIP LAY ANchored glimmered in the sunlight like blue crystal.

As the longboats rowed to shore, a crowd gathered. Various traders set out their goods. Trappers were selling fur skins, and the vaqueros—Mexican cowboys—had stacks of cowhides. There was also a small group of peasants watching the longboats pull in. Although the peasants had been paid to be there, they seemed unhappy.

A knot of caballeros stood a short distance from the others. They were rich and powerful ranchers dressed in their silver-trimmed finery. All were waiting to greet the former governor, Don Rafael Montero.

When the first longboat reached the beach, a lone figure stepped forward out of the crowd. Don Luis had aged, and one eye was milky, but he still carried himself erect. As Montero stepped out of the longboat, Don Luis lifted his arms.

"The governor has returned!" he announced. "Welcome home, Don Rafael. It has been too long."

"Thank you, Don Luis," Montero said, embracing him.

Don Luis lowered his voice. "You once said that you favored me above all. Consider this a fool's apology for ever doubting you." He slipped a small pouch into Montero's hand.

When Montero opened the pouch he saw a rough nugget the size of an egg—pure gold. He gave Don Luis a sly smile.

Don Luis spoke up so the others could hear. "Come. A crowd has gathered to greet you."

Dutifully the peasants shuffled forward. But they showed very little enthusiasm. At Don Luis's signal a band began to play a rousing march. The finely dressed ranchers began clapping and cheering as they hurried to greet Montero.

But one man was not smiling as he pushed his way past the onlookers. The man moved quickly despite his slight limp. Diego de la Vega—once known as Zorro—edged closer to his enemy. In his belt was the dagger he had used to cut himself out of his grave. Diego's eyes shone with a single desire—to kill Montero.

"Don Peralta, you're looking well," Montero said, greeting the nobleman at the head of the crowd.

Montero finished shaking hands with the aristocrats and looked out at the crowd. He gestured for the few who were still clapping to stop.

"Please," he said crisply. "I know you're not really happy to see me, so let's stop pretending, shall we?"

Shocked, the nobles traded anxious glances. The traders and farmers in the crowd were also bewildered.

There was a long moment of silence. Then a rough female voice in the crowd spoke up.

"Would it help if we chanted your name?" the voice jeered. "Viva Montero! Viva Montero!"

There was a chorus of raucous laughter. The chanting became more of a taunt. The wealthy ranchers were fuming, but Montero met the challenge with a warm, relaxed smile.

"Go ahead—you have a right to laugh!" Montero told the crowd. "I know you've been paid—even threatened—to come out in the hot sun to greet me."

"No, no, no, Don Rafael!" Don Luis sputtered. "These people have the greatest respect—"

"Do not flatter me, Don Luis," Montero said with a playful smile. "They have no reason to respect me." He turned to the crowd. "And let me tell you this: I understand how you feel."

He had their attention. Even the musicians had stopped playing and were listening. Poised to strike, Diego kept moving closer, his eyes fixed on Montero.

"Why should you care about *any* of your leaders, past or present?" Montero went on, playing to his audience. "The Spanish oppressed you. The Mexicans ignored you. The ranchers . . . well, they seem content merely to cheat you."

The noblemen gaped at him in stunned silence.

"In fact, who, may I ask, has ever helped you?" Montero asked.

"Zorro!" a voice answered. "Zorro fought for the people!"

Diego froze at the familiar voice, glancing around. Then he saw him. Time hadn't diminished Fray Felipe's big moon face. The robust monk was as outspoken as ever.

Montero also froze at the mention of Zorro's name and the enthusiastic cheers it stirred up. But despite a stab of fear he stayed calm and kept talking.

"And where is he now, Padre?" Montero replied. "Your masked friend hasn't shown himself for twenty years."

There was a general murmur of agreement in the crowd. Diego edged closer to Montero, searching for an opening.

"People of California," Montero went on, "we can no longer trust our welfare to absent leaders and vanished heroes. It is time to take our destiny in our own hands, not as Spaniards, not as Mexicans . . . but as Californians!"

A healthy round of applause rose up from the crowd. The only man not smiling was Diego. Unable to find a good angle of attack, he was about to try a desperate long shot.

"I come before you with no mask," Montero said, confident he had won the crowd over. "Only the solemn pledge—a *real* pledge—to help you fight for a free and independent California!"

Montero's speech received a rousing ovation. Everyone was applauding and cheering, except for two men. One of them was Fray Felipe. The other was Diego de la Vega.

Diego's face was also grim as he got ready to strike. Just then a trio of ranchers clustered around Montero, blocking Diego.

Another moment of life, Diego thought, but soon

Montero dies. He stepped behind Montero and waited for a squat bulldog of a man to get out of the way.

"With all due respect, sir," Don Hector said in a hoarse whisper, "we'd be crushed if we tried to start a war with Santa Anna."

Montero beamed and whispered back, "But of course."

The ranchers looked at one another, confused but interested. Don Hector stepped away from Montero, giving Diego a window of attack. The time had come.

Diego drew his arm back, knife glinting in the sunlight.

"Father?"

The female voice stopped Diego's arm in midstrike. It sounded exactly like Esperanza's. Both he and Montero turned at the same time. Diego blinked in disbelief.

He almost fainted when he saw her. Coming toward him was his beloved Esperanza. Then slowly it dawned on Diego's stunned brain. The young woman was Elena—his daughter.

As if in a trance, Diego watched her come near. He half expected her to recognize him, reach out and embrace him, but of course she walked right past the aged Diego. She brushed his shoulder as she hurried into the waiting arms of Montero.

"Gentlemen," Montero announced proudly. "Allow me to introduce my daughter, Elena."

Someone in the now-friendly crowd handed Elena a bouquet. Elena smiled and smelled the flowers. A strange expression came over her face. "Can anyone tell me what this flower is? It smells so familiar."

Diego knew—they were the same flowers that had

hung over her crib twenty years before—but he was unable to speak. He had not seen his daughter since the night her mother was murdered.

Don Luis stepped forward. "Yes, senorita—it's romania. But it grows only in California, and I believe this is your first visit to our shores."

Elena smelled the flowers again, haunted by a strange feeling. The scent was so familiar. . . .

Diego recognized Elena's expression. It was the same one Esperanza had worn when she was confused. Overcome by raging emotions, he let the dagger fall from his hand.

He knew he could not kill Montero, destroy his hated enemy, because Elena had come to love him. She depended on Montero as a father. Defeated, drained, and racked with despair, Diego turned away. The ragged gray figure lingered for a last glance at his beloved daughter, then vanished like a ghost.

The cantina was little more than two walls and a straw roof. There was a crude wooden bar that served whiskey and beer. The few chairs and tables all had a wide-open view of the dusty street.

Alejandro sat at one of the tables, bleary-eyed and half drunk. He banged his empty glass down. "More whiskey! Or whatever you call this."

The bartender carried a bottle over to Alejandro's table.

"Keep it full," Alejandro growled, pushing the glass at him. "I don't want to see the bottom of this glass."

The bartender shrugged. "Money first."

Fuming, Alejandro dug into his pockets, muttering to

himself. His hands came up empty. The bartender shook his head and moved away. Desperate, Alejandro grabbed his arm.

"What about this?"

Alejandro showed the bartender Joaquin's medallion. The bartender studied it. "Silver?" he asked doubtfully.

"Of course silver!" Alejandro blustered. "The finest, uh, Corinthian silver. Can't you tell?"

The bartender scratched his mustache, still doubtful. Corinthian or not, it looked like real silver, worth at least one more drink. He filled Alejandro's glass, then reached for the medallion.

A bony hand closed around the medallion.

The bartender looked up angrily. Diego's burning eyes stared at the bartender. He stood there, leaning on a cane, the medallion dangling from his fingers, as if daring the bartender to take it.

The savage glint in the old man's eyes convinced the bartender to back off. Diego glanced warily at Alejandro.

"Where did you get this?"

Alejandro ignored him and gulped his drink. "It was my brother's," he said finally. "He's dead."

Diego nodded. "I'm sorry."

"You're sorry?" Alejandro snorted. "Why should you be sorry?"

Diego knew exactly how he felt—the bitterness, the awful loneliness, the clawing anger. He'd been there and back. Twice. But he also knew it was useless to tell Alejandro. Instead he examined the medallion carefully. He noticed a tiny bloodstain on the face. "You shouldn't trade something like this for a mere glass of whiskey."

Alejandro raised his eyebrows. "Why not? You think I could get two?"

He laughed loudly at his own bad joke, banging the table. Suddenly the laughter froze in his mouth. He sat bolt upright, staring as if he'd just seen some terrible demon.

An icy chill sliced Alejandro's belly like a razor when he saw Captain Love across the square. Without a word he rose, picked up his sword, and started outside.

Diego grabbed his shoulder. "Who is that?"

"The man who killed my brother."

Alejandro pushed past the old man, but Diego threw him back against the wall. Alejandro blinked. The crazy old geezer was strong.

"You're drunk, and you're angry," Diego said calmly. "You're in no condition to fight a professional soldier."

"Get out of my way, old man," Alejandro warned. He glanced outside. The square was empty. Love was nowhere in sight.

"He's gone. You stupid old fool!" Alejandro ranted. "I've lost him!"

Diego lifted his cane and pressed it lightly against Alejandro's chest. "Maybe you would like to demonstrate your skill on me."

Alejandro's grief and frustration boiled over into murderous rage. He lunged at Diego with his sword. Flicking his cane, Diego swept the blade aside and nimbly stepped back so that Alejandro spun around and fell flat on his butt.

Furious now, Alejandro got up slowly, then charged without warning. Like a bullfighter, Diego barely moved. He blocked the sword thrust with his cane and, with one quick move, picked Alejandro's blade right out of his hand.

Diego caught the sword in midair. As Alejandro barreled past, he whacked him with the cane, knocking Alejandro into a wall and down to the floor.

Diego loomed over the fallen Alejandro and smiled. "Would you care to try again?"

Totally outfought, Alejandro just gave a small shake of his head.

"You're welcome," Diego said.

Alejandro stiffly got up. "For what?"

"Saving your life."

Alejandro's rage flared up. "I would have killed him!"

"Not on this day." Diego sighed. "He is trained to kill. You seem trained to drink. You would have fought bravely . . ."

Alejandro nodded, puffing up his chest.

". . . and died quickly. Who then would avenge your brother?"

Diego's question stung Alejandro's pride. "I would have found a way," he boasted. "I have never lost a fight."

Diego smiled. "Except to a crippled old man."

There was nothing Alejandro could say. He looked away, embarrassed.

Diego leaned closer. "There is a saying, 'When the pupil is ready, the master will appear.' If you want to kill this man, I can teach you how—how to move, how to think. How to take your revenge *and* live to celebrate it." Diego met Alejandro's eyes. "It will take dedication and time. But will your enemy be any less dead if you kill him later?"

"Why are you so eager to help me?"

Diego knelt beside Alejandro and carefully looped the medallion around his neck. "Because you once did the same for me."

Slowly it dawned on Alejandro as he recalled that day so long ago. He stared hard at the old man's face—the fierce eyes, the curved mouth. Alejandro sat up straight.

"You're Zorro," he said in an awed whisper.

Diego didn't reply.

"I thought you were dead."

A dark curtain fell over Diego's eyes.

"I was," he said softly.

6

RAFAEL MONTERO'S VAST ESTATE HAD BEEN WELL CARED for while he was away. The gardens were manicured, and the huge house sparkled like a king's palace.

Near the outer wall an obstacle course had been set up to amuse Montero's guests. Two mounted men, Captain Love and another rider, galloped between two lines of wooden posts. On each post was a pumpkin. As the riders raced past, their swords sliced the pumpkins that sat atop the posts.

Both riders showed great skill with sword and horse as they thundered toward the finish line.

There were two spectators. Montero and Don Luis walked across the lush lawns. Montero studied a guest list while keeping one eye on the horse race.

"This is a tentative guest list," Don Luis explained. "All the ranchers have responded, save Lara and Obregon."

Montero snorted. "See that they do. I want every landowner in California at this banquet."

"As you wish," Don Luis said. He put away the list.

The two men continued their stroll, still watching the contest in the distance.

"There's something else I need you to do for me, Luis," Montero said casually. He leaned closer. "I want you to pay a visit to General Santa Anna."

Don Luis stopped in his tracks. "Santa Anna?"

"Let him know that I've arrived and that we'll contact him in a few days."

Don Luis frowned. "I don't understand, Rafael. Why alert Santa Anna to your presence?"

Montero's casual manner stiffened. "Please, Luis," he snapped. "Don't question everything I ask you to do." He turned his attention to the climax of the contest. "Just do it."

Captain Love was riding hard, his opponent right on his heels. They charged for the finish line. Love narrowly won.

Montero squinted at the second rider in disbelief. The skillful swordsman was none other than his daughter, Elena!

Furious, Montero marched toward Elena, who was being congratulated by Captain Love. From the sheepdog look on his usually stony face, it was obvious Captain Love was taken by the lovely young woman.

"Well done, Miss Montero," Love said politely. "You very nearly won."

Elena gave him a playful smile. "I barely kept up."

Though she clearly needed no help, Love hurried to assist Elena down from the saddle. "No, no," he insisted, "you ride brilliantly."

Flattered, Elena gave him a dazzling smile.

"Thank you, Captain."

Montero approached, fuming with anger. Love was too intent on Elena to notice.

"Your daughter is an excellent rider, Don Rafael . . . considering that she is a woman."

Elena bristled at his comment. Her father was also upset, for his own reasons.

"I'm glad you found her *worthy* of competition, Captain Love," Montero said, his voice heavy with sarcasm. "Perhaps next time you'd like to wrestle with her?"

Love blinked uncertainly.

"Father!" Elena said, shocked.

"Sir, I—I meant no disrespect," Love stammered. "I—"

Montero cut him off. "I hired you to run my army, Captain Love. Not to encourage my daughter to embarrass herself in public."

"Father, please. I challenged *him!"* Elena cried.

Montero continued to glare accusingly at Love.

Elena took her father by the arm. "I apologize, Captain Love." Head high, she firmly led her father away.

They walked silently for a few moments. Then Montero bent closer to his daughter. "You let him win, of course?" he murmured.

A slow smile broke through Elena's frown.

"Of course."

Unlike Montero's estate, Diego's secret cave had been neglected for the past twenty years. Everything was decayed, rusted, or broken.

But a few things had withstood the ravages of time. The raised marble floor shaped like a circle was still intact. So was a tall ship's mast, its spars and jib boom held in place by rigging ropes. The network of ropes looked like a huge spiderweb. The structure was designed to increase a climber's acrobatic agility and strength.

Diego slowly walked around, followed by an awestruck Alejandro. "I can't believe it," Alejandro whispered. "I never thought that one day I would be standing in the lair of the Fox."

Hesitantly, Alejandro mounted the short stairway and walked across the large marble circle. Underneath a coat of dust the floor's smooth stone surface was inlaid with a familiar design: circles within circles.

Alejandro lifted the medallion that hung around his neck. The silver pendant had the same circle pattern as the marble floor.

Diego began to wander about the cave, inspecting the effects of the passing years. He picked something up and blew the dust away. "When you were a child, Rafael Montero was governor of California." He looked at Alejandro. "Do you remember?"

"I remember," Alejandro said, meeting Diego's stare. "His soldiers killed many people, and he was the sworn enemy of Zorro."

Diego nodded. "Montero has come back. He has some design for California. Otherwise, he would not have hired your Captain Love. We must find out what that design is."

"And then what?" Alejandro pressed.

Diego smiled. "Then, if you are ready, we will both tempt our fate."

Inflamed by the mention of the hated Captain Love, Alejandro drew his sword. "Let's go, then!"

"Do you know how to use that thing?"

"The pointy end goes into the other man," Alejandro snapped, insulted by the question.

Diego heaved a long sigh. "This will take a lot of work."

Drawing his sword, he stepped onto the raised marble circle and faced Alejandro. "This is the training circle of the Spanish Sword School. This circle will be your world, your whole life," Diego announced, "until I tell you otherwise."

With his sword Diego traced a large circle in the dust. "Outside of the circle . . ." He paused and looked up, eyes like black flames. "There is nothing outside of it."

"Captain Love is outside of it," Alejandro muttered, still brooding over his brother's murder.

"There is *nothing* outside of it," Diego said sharply. "Until I tell you, Captain Love does not exist!"

Diego took a deep breath and softened his tone. "Revenge can be a cruel master. It may seem to inspire you, but in the end it will cloud your judgment—and betray your attack."

As he spoke, Diego began to move in ever-tightening circles. "As your skill with the sword improves, you will progress to a smaller circle. With each new circle you move that much closer to your enemy, that much closer to justice."

Alejandro grinned, totally fascinated. "I like this part," he said. He spoke too soon.

Diego walked closer to Alejandro. Casually he lifted his sword. He placed the tip directly in the center of the medallion hanging around Alejandro's neck.

The innermost circle.

"You will move to this circle," Diego instructed, "the perfect striking distance. Where there is no time to see and react. Where you can rely only on your training, instincts, and speed."

Diego lifted his sword. "Shall we?"

Those two words kicked off the most grueling challenge of Alejandro's young life. Each day brought a new form of torture.

There was the beam. The idea was to walk across a narrow beam of wood. On either side of the beam were heavy sacks of grain hanging from wooden poles. The sacks swung like padded clubs across the beam.

Alejandro paused to let one pass in front of him. Then he hopped forward, narrowly ducking the bag whizzing past his face. He jumped again—but too late. A heavy bag thumped him solidly on the skull, and Alejandro went sprawling.

Practicing sword-fighting with Diego was no less painful. It was actually more like a brawl. Relying on raw strength against his teacher, Alejandro attacked.

Diego sidestepped and whacked him across the stomach. As Alejandro doubled over, Diego's boot sent him crashing to the floor, gasping for air like a stunned fish.

Then there was the whip test. Alejandro stood at the edge of the outer circle. Diego stood at the center. Alejandro lunged and held his position. Diego cracked his whip and snapped a button off Alejandro's shirt. Much too close.

Alejandro tried again. This time Diego's whip cut his sleeve. Still too close. Alejandro moved back and measured the distance.

The next time, Diego's whip cracked an inch short of Alejandro's fingers. Perfect position.

But even after a few weeks Alejandro couldn't get the better of Diego in a sword fight. Using all his power, Alejandro attacked strongly, moving Diego back a foot or so. *Crang!* Alejandro's sword was knocked from his grasp and sent spinning across the floor.

The worst exercise of all was Diego's test of strength. Twice a day Alejandro would position himself facedown between two wooden rails. He had to arch his back and support his body weight on his fingertips alone. Below him were two burning candles. Each time he sagged an inch, the flames would put a fresh scar on his chest.

To make sure he did everything correctly, Diego would sit beside him, legs resting comfortably on Alejandro's back. Ignoring Alejandro's yells when he got too close to the flames, Diego continued reading his book.

As time went on, Alejandro's skills improved. He learned to time his moves, to dodge, to counterattack, but in the end Diego always won. However, Diego was finding it more and more difficult.

Just when Alejandro thought he'd mastered control, Diego introduced a new test. He cut several small squares of cloth. He held one up next to the wall and dropped it. Alejandro lunged with his sword—and missed. Diego dropped another. Alejandro missed it.

On the fourth try, Alejandro nailed it—pinning the cloth square to the wall. On the fifth try, he did it again.

After weeks of intense training, Alejandro was becoming an expert. He moved at incredible speed around the training circle, sword flashing as he countered Diego's thrusts. Suddenly, with a flurry of graceful sword strokes, Alejandro plucked Diego's sword out of the air—just as Diego had taken his the day they met.

"Well?" Alejandro said, unable to hide his pleased grin.

Diego finally gave him a small smile. "Maybe one day you will make a swordsman."

Alejandro felt as if he'd just been awarded a medal.

Diego crossed the room to the table where he kept his sacred objects: his heavy gold cross and jeweled rosary as well as a pair of carved gold candleholders. Without a word he scooped the objects into a plain brown sack.

"What are you doing?" Alejandro asked. "Aren't those—"

Diego shrugged impatiently. "They mean nothing. They're trinkets. I'll trade them for food and drink. All that matters is that we keep going."

The intensity in his voice cut off any further protest, but Alejandro knew how much the objects meant to Diego. They were his only link to his past.

After long weeks of training in the cave, it was a real treat to go to town. Alejandro had shaved his beard for the occasion. Without it he looked nothing like his picture on the wanted poster.

Diego, too, was well disguised, with his white hair and simple clothing. He drove a small mule-drawn wagon into the town square. Alejandro lay slumped in the back, his hat pulled low over his face. The sack of sacred objects sat beside him.

Both men lifted their heads when they heard the drumming of hoofbeats behind them.

A corporal and two soldiers were leading five unbroken horses along the street. Alejandro recognized the squat Corporal Garcia from their previous meeting.

As usual, the soldiers were arrogant, scattering peasants in their path as they rode into the town square.

But Alejandro's eyes were fixed on only one thing—the splendid black stallion Garcia was leading.

Without warning the stallion reared back, knocking Garcia out of his saddle.

Free from his rope, the stallion charged madly around the plaza, creating havoc among the vendors. Fruit baskets overturned, stalls collapsed, and people ran in every direction.

Diego sat calmly, gaze riveted on the rampaging stallion. "A black Andalusian," he said softly. "Magnificent."

"He looks like your old horse, Toronado."

Diego nodded. "Enough like him to be his ghost."

Some women screamed as the stallion kicked over a stall full of scarves and bright shawls. At the same time a carriage stopped nearby. Don Peralta and his wife stepped out of the carriage—directly into the path of the stampeding stallion!

The finely dressed couple froze in fear as the stallion charged straight at them, sharp hooves tearing up clouds of dirt.

7

INSTANTLY ALEJANDRO LEAPED OUT OF THE WAGON AND jumped directly between the stallion and the terrified couple. As if he had all the time in the world, Alejandro ushered the couple into the carriage, then whirled to face the stallion bearing down on him.

Alejandro lifted his hand and murmured some quiet sounds. The stallion stopped short and reared up high, hooves threatening to smash Alejandro's skull.

Unafraid, Alejandro whispered soothingly and stepped closer. As the stallion came back down on its front legs, Alejandro stroked its mane. He kept murmuring, as if putting a child to sleep. In a few moments the horse was as placid as a lamb.

Sputtering, Garcia struggled to his feet. Furious at having been publicly humiliated, he ran over to grab the stallion's lead rope. Shooting Alejandro a nasty glare, Garcia hauled the stallion back across the rubbled square.

Alejandro hardly noticed Garcia, still staring at the stallion. Behind him, Don Peralta stepped hesitantly out of his carriage. The elderly rancher was still trembling in fear.

"You, uh, you saved my life, young man," Peralta gasped.

Alejandro smiled politely. "My privilege, sir."

To show his gratitude Don Peralta reached into his pocket and flipped Alejandro his reward—the grand total of one peso.

Alejandro bowed grandly. "Thank you, your majesty."

Not sure if he was being insulted or not, Don Peralta took his wife's arm and hurried away.

As Alejandro bent to take his bow, he noticed all the brightly colored scarves blowing around the square. At that moment a black scarf wrapped itself around his ankle. He picked it up and walked slowly back to the wagon.

Diego wasn't pleased. "How could you be so careless? You're a wanted man. Anybody could have recognized you."

Alejandro flipped the peso to Diego. "It was worth it."

"Worth it for one lousy peso?"

With a mysterious smile Alejandro reached inside his shirt. Carefully, so as not to be seen, he pulled out a wallet, a ruby necklace, a gold ring, a diamond bracelet, and various other objects—all neatly lifted from Don Peralta and his wife while hustling them to safety.

"Maybe there are some things I can teach you, Don Diego," he said smugly. "I am not sure the pupil is ready"—his smile became a cocky grin—"but the master is here."

Then Alejandro's grin faded. He pointed at the sack containing Diego's sacred objects. "Now you can keep those trinkets of yours—the ones that mean nothing to you."

Alejandro dropped the entire haul, which included an official-looking document, into Diego's surprised hands. Twisting the black scarf around his fist, Alejandro moved away.

As Diego watched his pupil disappear into the crowd, he realized that Alejandro was ready to graduate.

The dark red sun sank low behind the bell tower, sending long shadows across the square. Slowly one of the shadows seemed to split apart and edge along a deserted side street.

Alejandro peered through the crude holes he'd cut in the black scarf. He knotted the scarf around his head. It wasn't much of a mask, but it would do the job.

His heart pounded like that of the young boy who'd cut through the undertaker's black canvas twenty years before. He thought of Joaquin. Soon his brother would be avenged. But first he had some business to clear up.

Alejandro took his time, waiting until dusk before making his move. He hid himself among some horses that stood hitched to a water trough. As he crept between them he glanced down and saw his reflection in the water.

He looked like Zorro himself!

Alejandro took a small bow. *"Buenas noches,* Zorro. You look better than ever."

Unfortunately he couldn't stop long to admire himself. He had to find the black stallion and claim it as his own.

Alejandro reached over and took a rope from a nearby saddle. As he turned, he was startled by a sudden flurry of hoofbeats. Someone was riding toward the hitching post, much too fast for Alejandro to avoid being seen.

Alejandro's hand dropped to his sword. He turned, ready for a fight, as the horseman pulled to a halt. Alejandro glanced up, and his heart stopped beating.

The rider was a beautiful young woman. She looked like a dark angel with her hair blown wild and her face glowing from the hard ride.

But if his angel screamed, Alejandro's new career would come to an abrupt end.

Surprisingly, Elena wasn't afraid when she saw the masked man. Despite the black scarf that covered half his face, she could tell he was quite handsome, with his black hair, strong chin, curved lips, and intense eyes.

As they stared at each other, Elena felt a shock of electricity pass between them. Then the masked man half smiled and put a finger to his lips.

"Shh."

Elena narrowed her eyes, ready to bolt at the first wrong move. Suddenly her horse whinnied and shuffled nervously. The masked man caught its bridle and whispered, "Shh," to the horse as well.

In spite of herself Elena smiled.

"Be careful, senorita," the masked man whispered. "There are dangerous men about."

"Well, if you see any, be sure to point them out," Elena said dryly.

The masked man smiled and slipped away. One moment he was there, the next he had melted into the shadows.

For long moments Elena sat there and scanned the darkness, half hoping he'd return. Finally she dismounted, tied her horse, and walked slowly toward the church.

By the time Elena was inside the gates, Alejandro had managed to reach the church roof. He still remembered the alleys, shortcuts, and hidden stairways he had discovered as a child.

From the roof he could see directly down into the horse corral. Sure enough, a lone soldier was leading the black stallion to the stables.

Luckily, Alejandro recalled a quick way inside the stables. He took a short running jump and landed lightly on the next roof.

The soldier leading the black stallion didn't hear anything. He was too busy making sure the stallion didn't get away from him. If that happened, Garcia would have his hide. Garcia didn't deserve a stallion like this, the soldier thought. The plump sergeant had trouble sitting on a mule.

The soldier secured the horse in a stall, then walked to a large door at the end of the stable that led to his barracks. Along the way the soldier passed the forge the blacksmith used to make horseshoes. The forge had a wide chimney to handle the blazing fire needed to melt iron, but at night there was no fire.

As the soldier opened the door to the barracks, Alejandro's head emerged upside down from the mouth of the chimney.

Alejandro watched the soldier exit through the door and shut it behind him. Then, using the rope he'd grabbed earlier, Alejandro lowered himself to the floor.

He peered through the gloom, checking the stalls. The

magnificent black stallion was there, standing stiffly at the rail, as if expecting him.

Taking a saddle and a bridle from a nearby stand, Alejandro cautiously moved toward the horse.

The stallion nervously stamped his hooves. The sound echoed inside the stable. Alejandro glanced at the barracks door, hand at his sword.

Nothing.

Alejandro moved closer to the stallion.

"Shh," he said, giving the horse a reassuring pat. "I have come to give you the great honor of being my horse."

The stallion eyed him suspiciously.

Gently Alejandro placed the saddle on the horse, then stepped back. He waited a few moments. The horse remained quiet.

Alejandro carefully buckled the saddle and put on the bridle. For a few seconds he stroked the horse's nose. He looked into the stallion's coal black eyes. He and the horse trusted each other.

They were ready.

He led the stallion out of the stall and prepared to mount. A muffled burst of laughter drifted through the door.

Alejandro put one foot in the stirrup and very gently mounted the horse. He sat astride the stallion's back and held his breath. The horse remained calm and serene.

"We are like one spirit," Alejandro whispered.

He nudged the horse with his heel.

It was a big mistake.

The horse exploded like a stack of fireworks. Crazily bucking and kicking, the stallion charged in every direction, trying to throw Alejandro off his back. When

THE YEAR: 1821

The spirit of justice demands a champion—El Zorro, the fox.

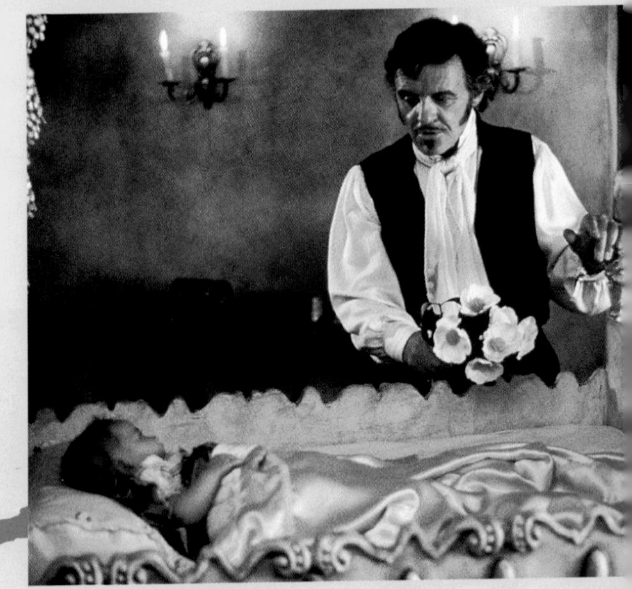

"But the good prince raced to the bridge, fighting off a hundred guards," Don Diego whispers to his sleeping daughter.

Rafael Montero, the evil governor of Alta California, comes to arrest Zorro—and destroy his life forever.

Twenty Years Later

Joaquin and Alejandro are wanted men . . .

. . . while Rafael Montero searches for his old enemy Don Diego in Talamantes Prison . . .

. . . then enjoys a festive welcome from his fellow aristocrats.

Alejandro begins his lessons to master the secrets of the sword.

Overwhelmed by her beauty, Alejandro magically presents a red rose to Elena.

At Montero's lavish party Alejandro and Elena dance.

BELOW:
"My friends, I give you the independent Republic of California," Montero announces.

Montero and Captain Harrison Love lead the way on a dusty journey to the secret gold mine.

At last, after all his hard work, Alejandro wears the mask of Zorro.

Don Diego's secret signal—the mark of Zorro!

"Whatever it is you stole from my father," Elena tells Zorro, "I want it back."

Determined to avenge his brother's death and free the slaves at the mine, Zorro battles Love.

Between two old enemies, a fight to the finish!

With the mine in flames, Zorro and Elena lead the exhausted slaves to freedom.

that failed, he crazily smashed against the wooden poles that supported the hayloft.

"Whoa!" Alejandro croaked, holding on for his life. "Whoa!"

Again the stallion rammed the support pole, and suddenly the platform collapsed! The entire structure—beams, loft, and heavy bales of hay—thundered down on Alejandro like a rockslide.

The barracks room where the soldiers were housed was quite noisy. It held about twenty soldiers, all relaxing after the day's work. Some were lying on bunks that were stacked against the wall. Others were cleaning their rifles.

At a long table in the center of the room, Sergeant Garcia sat playing cards with a group of soldiers. He was bellowing that he'd been cheated. The other cardplayers roared with laughter at their fat sergeant. Everyone knew Garcia was terrible at cards.

A sudden clap of thunder cut off their raucous shouts. They all fell silent as they listened to the commotion next door. Immediately Garcia lurched out of his chair and stumbled toward the stable, followed by the others.

But when they pushed open the door and charged inside, they faced full-scale destruction. Roaring straight at them—twisting and turning like a hairy tornado—was a monstrous haystack!

Instantly they all scrambled back and slammed the door behind them. Lopez and the soldiers raced for their rifles. As Lopez fumbled for the key to the weapons room, the others went for their swords. Those who'd been cleaning their rifles hastily put them back together.

Kraaaack! The huge stallion crashed through the door

in a spray of splintered wood, trailing hay like a shrieking black comet!

Clinging to the beast for dear life, Alejandro saw soldiers on all sides. But before any of them could recover, the stallion spun in midair, its hind legs lashing out, toppling soldiers everywhere.

Those still on their feet panicked and rushed to their bunks, in search of protective shelter. As if to show how wrong they were, the stallion reared up, throwing Alejandro to the floor. Front hooves flailing like sharp clubs, the stallion demolished the entire tier of bunks. Men, beds, planks, trunks—all came crashing down.

Meanwhile Alejandro sprang to his feet in the midst of the chaos. "Ah, you think you can do this without me," he muttered.

As the stallion's hooves came down, Alejandro jumped. He leaped into the saddle, turned the horse around, and headed for the outer door. With a giant vault, the stallion shattered the door and galloped into the night.

But on the way out, Alejandro's head hit the top beam of the door and he was smacked to the floor once again.

Dazed and horseless, Alejandro staggered to his feet as a group of soldiers rushed him, swords drawn.

Despite the odds, Alejandro's long weeks of training gave him the advantage. He drew his sword and disarmed two soldiers, then whacked another's pistol aside. The wild shot hit a fourth soldier.

Sword hissing, Alejandro fought his way to the open door. Then he noticed two soldiers running outside. Soon they would return with reinforcements.

Alejandro jumped aside to avoid a thrown sword and

found himself cornered by five soldiers. As he grimly fought them off, he saw more soldiers coming in.

He glimpsed an open door with only one man to pass: the plump sergeant. Garcia saw him coming and raised his pistol. *Bam!* He missed, wounding a man who was about to stab Alejandro in the back.

Alejandro knocked Garcia aside, lunged through the door, and slammed it behind him. Pushing hard against the soldiers trying to get in, Alejandro managed to bolt the door. He looked around. He'd barricaded himself in the weapons room.

Could be worse, he observed, looking over the pistols, rifles, and casks of gunpowder. There was even a small cannon.

Whack! The soldiers outside rammed the door. Another hit and the wooden bolt would give way.

There were too many to fight off with sword or pistol, Alejandro thought. He could get only three or four at most, which left him just one choice. He picked up a cask of gunpowder and began loading the cannon.

Wracckk! The wooden bolt cracked and was barely blocking the door. Quickly Alejandro rammed a cannonball into the thick iron barrel. He grabbed a burning torch from the wall as the door crashed open.

Kradoom! The cannon's blast filled the small room with smoke and heat. When the smoke cleared, Alejandro saw that the front wall of the building had been demolished. The soldiers were nowhere in sight.

Alejandro threw aside the torch that had fired the cannon and began to laugh. Even though he was covered with dirt and his crude mask was crooked, he'd won.

"The legend has returned!" Alejandro shouted.

Suddenly out of the corner of his eye he saw a bright light. The laughter caught in his throat. The torch he'd tossed away had ignited the gunpowder he'd spilled while loading the cannon.

Now the burning trail was streaking for the open cask of gunpowder. He knew he couldn't get out in time, so he did the next best thing.

Alejandro sprang, scooped up the cask of gunpowder, and sprinted toward the door. Unfortunately the cask kept spilling powder. When Alejandro glanced back, he saw that the brightly burning fuse was catching up to him!

8

"YOW!" YELLING, THE WOULD-BE ZORRO FLUNG THE gunpowder cask over his shoulder and charged full speed out of the barracks.

The cask rolled back into the weapons room, giving Alejandro an extra few seconds. He hit the outer wall running and scrambled to the top.

Whooom! The barracks erupted in a sheet of flame, hurling him to the hard ground. Dazed, he looked up. He was outside the wall. He could hear men yelling in the distance. By the light of the rising flames he saw the church a few yards ahead. The door was open.

Sanctuary, Alejandro told himself as he dashed across the square. He closed the church door behind him and looked for someplace to hide.

A large figure loomed up behind him. Alejandro whirled, ready to fight.

It was Fray Felipe. Alejandro lowered his sword. "Don't yell," he warned.

The monk scowled. "I'm too old to yell."

"I need sanctuary, Father. You don't know me but—"

Fray Felipe squinted at the rumpled masked man. Then his big moon face lit up. "Zorro?" he said, stunned. "Zorro! Of course I know you." He peered closer. "I must say the years have been far kinder to you than they have been to me. I remember that time you—"

"I'm sorry," Alejandro said curtly. "I have no time to talk now, Father. I need you to hide me, please."

At that moment they heard the sound of men shouting outside. Horses galloped across the square.

Fray Felipe moved to the door and slid the thick iron bolt into place. When he returned, his face was pink with excitement.

"It's just like the old days!" the monk said gleefully.

Someone banged on the door. Alejandro looked around for a hiding place. Then he saw the confessional booth near the altar.

The booth went from floor to ceiling and had a thick cloth roof. Quickly, Alejandro moved to the booth and slipped into the priest's compartment.

"Father? Is that you?" a female voice asked.

Alejandro froze. He said nothing, stunned that someone was in the booth.

"Padre? Is everything all right?"

She thought he was the priest. Alejandro shrank back, trying to hide. But the woman rapped on the partition between them. He had no choice. He slid the partition open.

"Oh. Uh, yes—everything is well," he said in a deep voice.

There was a black screen between them, which obscured their faces. But somehow the woman's voice sounded familiar.

"It sounds as if there's a battle going on out there," she said.

"Fear not, my dear," Alejandro said piously. "You are safe in the house of the lord."

"Those are wise words."

Alejandro put his hands together, enjoying the role of priest. "You think so? Thank you. I am very new at this."

For the first time the young woman, Elena Montero, realized something was strange. The priest was probably a new one from Spain, she thought. Considering the sins she had to confess, it was just as well he was a stranger.

"Forgive me, Father, for I have sinned. It's been three days since my last confession."

"Three days? How many sins could you have committed in three days?" Alejandro asked. "Maybe you should come back when you've had more time."

Elena was becoming quite confused. She had never heard a priest say such things. "Pardon me?"

Alejandro peered hard through the screen and caught his breath. Although the screen and shadows veiled the woman's features, he glimpsed her eyes, large and lovely. It was the lady he'd met at the hitching post.

"Just a small joke, senorita," he explained. "Tell me your sins."

"I have broken the Fourth Commandment, Father."

Alejandro rapidly counted on his fingers. "Ah, you stole something?"

"That's not the Fourth Commandment!" Elena snapped.

"Of course not," Alejandro said hastily. "What could I have been thinking?"

"I dishonored my father."

It was hard for Alejandro to believe the exquisite lady could commit any sin. "You dishonored your father? Well, maybe your father is a swine. Maybe he deserved to be dishonored."

For a moment she was silent.

"Just what kind of a priest are you?" Elena asked suspiciously.

"I told you, a very new one. Are you afraid of change, my child?"

"Not at all," she said proudly. "I welcome it."

Alejandro sat back. "Then please continue."

"I try to behave properly—the way my father would like me to. But I'm afraid my heart is too wild."

Wild. The word got Alejandro's attention.

"Too wild?" he repeated.

"I also . . ."

"Yes?"

"I had improper thoughts about a man."

"No!" Alejandro said in disbelief.

"I did. I think he was a bandit or something."

For the second time, Alejandro caught his breath.

"Really?" he said, his voice husky. "Black mask, deep voice, ruggedly handsome?"

"Yes. And when he looked at me—I mean, when I looked at him, Padre, I felt like—"

"Like the ocean was roaring in your ears?" Alejandro suggested, his heart racing.

"Yes, yes, but even more than that—warm, feverish . . ."

Zorro decided to explore the possibilities.

"Yearning?" he suggested innocently.

"Yearning," Elena admitted, looking away.

Zorro smiled, suddenly impressed with himself—and her. She had also felt the electricity. "I think we have a slightly new policy toward yearning," he declared.

"Really?" Elena said hopefully. Then she thought about it. "Wait a moment. 'A slightly *new* . . .'" She peered through the screen. "Who are you?"

A sudden crash diverted her attention. Alejandro heard footsteps and men shouting. Through the babble he recognized Captain Love's voice. He could never forget the man who'd murdered his brother.

Nor could he forgive, Alejandro thought grimly.

"Search the chapel, the loft, the rectory," Love barked. "All of it!"

"This is a house of God!" Fray Felipe protested as the sound of running boots echoed through the church.

Love took the news calmly. "Don't worry, Padre. We'll be gone by the time he gets back."

Hunched inside the confessional, Alejandro decided to get the young woman to safety. "Senorita," he whispered urgently, "you've done nothing wrong. Trust your heart. It won't lead you astray. Now go!"

Love and his men were tramping about the chapel when Elena stepped out of the confessional.

The soldiers paused, astonished. "Elena!" Love exclaimed. "What are you doing here?"

Elena shrugged. "I was confessing."

Love's moonstruck expression hardened. "To whom?" he growled, eyes narrowed. "The priest is here."

Drawing his pistol, he stepped in front of Elena. "Stand back, Elena. There's a dangerous bandit loose."

"So I've heard," Elena said, trying to control her skidding emotions. Her shock and horror crashed like runaway trains when Love fired point-blank into the confessional.

Love's soldiers joined in with a barrage of gunfire. Elena gasped, on the edge of fainting. No one could have survived that assault.

Everyone stood frozen in the silence. The gun smoke hung in the candlelight like funeral ribbons. Slowly the confessional door creaked open, its hinges shot away.

Empty.

Elena drew a long breath of relief. Love peered inside the confessional. Then he looked up.

There was a ragged hole in the cloth roof.

Unwilling to vent his rage in front of Elena, Captain Love glared at Fray Felipe. "Out of respect for Miss Montero, I will deal with you later."

The old monk scowled, trying to conceal his excitement. His prayers had been answered.

Zorro had returned.

A few feet above the chapel a masked figure crawled along the edge of the roof, searching for a way out.

He glanced down and paused. There below, calmly munching grass, was the black stallion. The horse stood in an alley behind the church only a yard or two away.

Alejandro was elated. His escape was at hand.

"Pssst! Horse! Come here!" he whispered loudly.

The horse kept eating.

Alejandro tried some other names. "Thunder! Blackie! Estúpido!"

The horse didn't even look up.

"Get over here! Now!" Alejandro commanded. "I warn you, I'll get another horse!"

The horse was unimpressed.

Frustrated, Alejandro let out a whistle.

The horse's ears pricked up. He looked at Alejandro, then walked to a spot directly below him.

Smiling proudly, Alejandro jumped off the roof onto the stallion's back—except that as Alejandro jumped, the horse took two easy steps forward.

The great horseman landed squarely on his butt!

The stallion turned his head and gave Alejandro a sleepy grin. Alejandro glared back.

The sound of muffled voices pulled him off the ground. Alejandro got to his feet and smoothly leaped over the horse's rump—into the saddle.

Once he was on the stallion's back, Alejandro let out a triumphant laugh. He'd done it. Digging his heels into the stallion's sides, he charged into the square.

Alejandro leaned over the horse's long neck, urging the stallion forward through the flaming chaos. Soldiers fired shots as they passed, but the stallion flew like the wind, hooves barely touching ground.

When he was clear of the square, Alejandro paused for a moment in front of an adobe wall. Three quick slashes and his blade carved a *Z* in the wall.

Then he wheeled his horse and galloped into the night.

9

WITH THE TIP OF HIS SWORD, DIEGO IDLY TRACED circles in the dust as he sat in the secret cave, waiting for Alejandro. The sound of hoofbeats roused his interest.

Diego looked up and saw Alejandro come riding into the cave astride the black stallion. He was dressed as a crude, ragged version of Zorro. All in all, Diego thought, he looked like a fatheaded fool. The mask was ridiculous, as was Alejandro's smug expression. Clearly Alejandro was expecting a parade in his honor, with flowers and a marching band.

"What do you think?" Alejandro demanded, striking a heroic pose.

Diego smiled and shook his head. "Truly remarkable. I would not have believed it."

"I got the black stallion. I carved a *Z* in the town square," Alejandro boasted. "The people will be speaking the name of Zorro again, Don Diego."

Deep rage clouded Diego's smile. "But all they will see is a fool! You steal a horse, you scribble on a wall, and you think you are worthy to wear that mask?" He ripped the mask from Alejandro's face and threw it to the floor.

Alejandro was stunned and angry. "Careful, old man."

"Zorro was not a show-off, a seeker of fame," Diego spat. "He was a servant of the people. He did what was needed."

Diego tried to push his way past Alejandro, but the young apprentice would not have it.

"And now he is needed again," Alejandro pleaded. "I didn't ask for your help in the cantina. But I came here to learn how to fight like you, to have your strength, your courage. Now when I try to use them, you slap me down. I'm tired of your training and your lecturing. Tired of waiting for you to tell me I'm ready. I have my own scores to settle, a new life to find. I thought I could do it here, but I was wrong."

The old master stared at his pupil. He was impressed with what he saw. Fire, determination, pride—all the right qualities for a new Zorro. But he was still crude, Diego thought.

"Choose your weapon."

Slightly confused, Alejandro slowly drew his sword and waved it at Diego. With a dramatic flourish Diego lifted a silver soup spoon. His other hand held a rolled-up parchment.

Alejandro recognized the parchment as part of the haul he'd lifted from the stingy Don Peralta. He lowered his sword.

"I don't understand."

Diego smiled. "Montero has invited every aristocrat in California to a banquet at his hacienda." He pointed the parchment at Alejandro. "But this is more than a social occasion. It must involve his plans for California somehow."

Diego's smile faded. "If you really want to be of service, you will join the guests—as a spy."

Diego's last three words flapped around Alejandro's brain like startled bats. He shook his head. "I can pass as Zorro. I could never pass as a nobleman."

"Then I must give you something that is now completely beyond your reach," Diego declared.

"What's that?"

"Charm."

Alejandro wasn't convinced. "And what will that do for me?"

Diego took a deep breath. "If you can convince Montero that you are a gentleman of stature, he will let you into his circle."

Alejandro took the delicate silver spoon from Diego's hand. He examined it as if it were a strange weapon. He tried to hold it between his fingers, but it slipped to the floor.

Alejandro sighed. "This is going to take a lot of work."

It was a grand party.

Guests came from far and wide to Rafael Montero's fabulous estate. The women arrived in coaches, the men riding beside them. Finely dressed grooms attended to the coaches, and personal servants trailed after the bejeweled guests.

Alejandro—now calling himself Don Alejandro—arrived on his newly acquired stallion, Toronado. Don

Alejandro was dressed in silver-trimmed finery that matched the stallion's rich saddle.

Behind him was his servant, Diego, riding a donkey. Diego dismounted and hurried to help his "master" down from his horse.

Alejandro took a deep breath. "This is definitely the most foolish thing I've ever done."

"I doubt that," Diego muttered to himself.

"We'll never get away with it," Alejandro told Diego.

Diego calmly brushed the road dust from Alejandro's blue velvet jacket. "Yes, we will," he insisted. "A nobleman is nothing more than a man who says one thing while thinking another."

To illustrate, Diego made a deep bow. "What a pleasure to see you," he said in a mild voice. Then his voice became a growl. "In a coffin, perhaps."

"And what if Montero recognizes you?" Alejandro demanded.

"He thinks himself a true nobleman. He would never look a servant in the face." Diego turned toward Montero's great house. "Good luck, Alejandro. And most of all, remember—do not let the other guests leave the table without you."

When they reached the front door a servant took Alejandro's invitation. Montero stood inside the hall, greeting his guests. He looked composed, almost radiant, as if his moment had arrived.

"Good evening, Don Rafael," Alejandro said, extending his hand. "I am Alejandro del Castillo y Garcia."

He took Montero's hand, dipped one knee, and bowed his head in greeting. The look on Montero's face told him that the older man was both surprised and pleased.

"I haven't seen that gesture in years—the formal greeting of the Spanish court."

Alejandro gave Diego a quick glance of triumph. "My father was very strict in matters of etiquette."

"And who was your father?"

"Don Bartolo del Castillo."

Montero's eyes narrowed as he studied his unknown guest. "I know of Don Bartolo, but I never had the pleasure of meeting him."

Calmly Alejandro held out his hand. Diego carefully placed an official document in it.

"My servant, Bernardo." Alejandro yawned.

As Diego had predicted, Montero didn't bother to look. He was more interested in the document Alejandro handed him.

"I arrived last week from Spain, by way of Paris, Lisbon, and San Francisco." Alejandro explained. "I am inspecting my family's holdings."

Montero nodded, unrolling the document.

"Queen Isabel of Spain has been very generous to us," Alejandro said with a modest shrug. "I have had recent correspondence with Her Royal Highness, as well as Queen Mother Maria Cristina."

Montero remained suspicious. "Very impressive," he said coldly, returning the document. "And what brings you to my door?"

Alejandro gave him a dazzling smile. "Her Royal Highness speaks highly of your earlier work in California." Such as looting and killing, Alejandro thought behind his polite words—just like a nobleman.

As expected, Montero couldn't resist royal recognition. A small smile broke through his stern expression.

"Really? Since California was lost to Mexico, I was under the impression I was out of favor with the Spanish court."

"That was clearly no fault of yours. Her Majesty told me this province is still a land of opportunity—for a man of vision."

Montero's smile faded a bit. "And you're a man of vision?"

"I'm a man in search of a vision."

Alejandro's answer seemed to please Montero. His smile widened and he nodded.

"But my timing is unfortunate," Alejandro said, looking around. "I seem to have interrupted a party. Perhaps I could call again?" He took a step backward.

"Please," Montero said warmly, "it would honor me if you joined us."

Alejandro bowed. "It would honor me to do so, sir."

Behind him Diego beamed proudly. His pupil had passed with flying colors.

"May I present my daughter, Elena."

Diego's emotions overturned like a sinking ship. He bit his lip, then looked up. Elena looked glorious. He turned away, overcome.

Alejandro's eyes never left Elena's as he kissed her hand. "Charmed," he said lightly. "I'm afraid I've brought no gift for the hostess. Oh, wait a moment!"

Alejandro plucked something out of the air. A red rose appeared in his hand. With a flourish he presented it to Elena.

"Thank you." Elena gave him a radiant smile, obviously pleased by the little magic trick. Even Diego was impressed.

Alejandro nodded, turned, and strolled casually into the house. Without looking back he snapped his fingers at his "servant."

"Bernardo! Pick up your feet!" he commanded, flaunting his newfound power.

Teeth clenched, Diego hurried after him.

Alejandro was enjoying himself immensely.

An orchestra played festive music. Guests sat at candlelit tables while servants brought them food and drink. Elegant couples danced with old-fashioned formality. Alejandro sat among the rich and spoiled, drinking expensive champagne. Too much champagne, in fact.

As the gentlemen around him talked stiffly of politics or local gossip, Alejandro lifted his empty glass.

"Bernardo! More champagne!"

Diego hurried to refill Alejandro's glass. As he poured, he muttered under his breath, "You overplay your part, *Don* Alejandro. Rein yourself in before you fall offstage. And watch the way you hold the glass!"

Alejandro pretended to cover a yawn. "I must say, I like you as a servant. It brings out your better qualities. By the way, there's a spot on my shoe," he added loudly. "Attend to it. Right away!"

Fuming, Diego got down on all fours to wipe away the spot. Alejandro turned and saw Elena approaching his table.

"It's not coming out!" Alejandro snapped. "Get the polish, and be quick about it!" He rolled his eyes. "Aye, the burdens of wealth."

"Yes, sir," Diego grunted, moving off.

"Don Alejandro," Elena said formally, "my father and I would like you to join us at our table."

Alejandro stood and offered her his arm. "I would be delighted, senorita."

Lingering nearby, Diego watched them go. He needed to go with them somehow, if only to make sure Alejandro didn't get carried away with his new image.

Glancing around the courtyard, he spotted a tray with glasses of wine on it.

Diego scooped up the tray and carried it into Montero's house as he trailed Alejandro.

At the great carved wood table in Montero's lavish dining room, the most powerful guests were having a lively discussion. As Alejandro approached with Elena, Montero rose from his seat.

"Ah, Don Alejandro," Montero greeted him. He gestured to the men seated around him. "Gentlemen, may I introduce Alejandro del Castillo y Garcia, recently arrived from Spain. I hope he will become a valued member of our circle."

Alejandro bowed to the assembled guests, who nodded in return. When he glanced at Captain Love, pure hatred flickered across his polite smile.

Montero saw it. "And this is Captain Harrison Love. Although not a nobleman, he is a man of kindred spirit."

There was an electric snap of tension as Alejandro shook Love's hand. Diego held his breath. Would Alejandro shed his aristocratic charm?

"Ah, Captain Love," Alejandro said thoughtfully. "Weren't you recently in pursuit of some legendary bandit?"

Love gave him a cool smile. "He was hardly legendary."

Alejandro flicked some dust from his jacket. "Oh, then, you captured him?"

The question caught Love off guard. "It's only a matter of time."

Alejandro shrugged. "Well, the bandit may have escaped, but the rest of us will think twice before going to confession."

The others around the table laughed, including Elena. Burning with anger and jealousy, Love shot Alejandro a glance of murderous hatred. But Alejandro didn't seem to notice, being occupied with helping Elena to her chair.

Love clenched his jaw. He would wait for a more favorable time to deal with this upstart.

Giddy with success, Alejandro glanced around for his "servant," but Diego was nowhere in sight.

Diego was on a private mission.

He was conducting an informal search of Montero's house, hoping to find something he could use against his sworn enemy.

His heartbeat was racing as he roamed the deserted halls, knowing he risked capture if anyone saw him.

Diego turned a corner. Ahead stood an armed sentry. He was guarding a large, heavy door.

Without missing a step, Diego continued down the hall, holding his drink tray high. As he swept past the guard, Diego noticed another door facing the armed sentry.

He walked briskly to the end of the hall and turned left. Once out of sight he stepped into a doorway. After making sure he was not observed, he opened the door and entered a darkened room.

Moving carefully, Diego crossed to another door. According to his calculations, this was the door that faced the guard. Diego peered through the crack.

Sure enough, there he was.

Casually, Diego tipped over the drinks tray, sending wineglasses crashing to the floor.

Squinting through the crack, Diego could see the guard's startled reaction. The man's eyes bulged wide at the sound of shattering glass.

Gripping his pistol, the guard crossed the hall and cautiously turned the knob. Diego stepped back, his heavy silver tray raised high, as the guard slowly entered.

Whack! Diego's silver tray connected with the guard's skull. Diego caught him before he hit the floor, then dragged his unconscious body behind a couch.

A moment later Diego appeared in the doorway, holding a set of keys. Within seconds he had unlocked the large door and slipped inside.

10

ALEJANDRO WAS FINDING IT DIFFICULT TO KEEP HIS EYE on Montero and Elena at the same time. Since Captain Love was keeping Elena occupied, Alejandro turned to Montero.

He glimpsed Montero whispering something to Don Luis. Alejandro pretended to sip his wine as Montero gave Don Luis a key. As the elderly gentleman left the table, Montero turned to his other guests.

Love was still talking to Elena, so Alejandro leaned closer to Montero for a private conversation.

"Captain Love is a very interesting man, Don Rafael," Alejandro observed. "Where did you find him?"

"In Morocco. Fighting for Spain in the campaign against the French."

"Ah . . ." Alejandro glanced away as if embarrassed. "A mercenary."

His superior air made Montero slightly uncomfortable. "Well, yes," he admitted. "But a fine soldier. Precise . . . and ruthless."

"Not exactly the type to settle down and raise a family."

Montero seemed puzzled. "Meaning what, exactly?"

Alejandro nodded toward Love and Montero's daughter. "He and Elena are clearly smitten with each other. I would have thought—"

"Captain Love may be smitten, Don Alejandro," Montero snapped, "but my daughter is quite another matter." He looked at Alejandro. "She will marry appropriately."

"A nobleman of Spanish lineage?" Alejandro suggested.

"Exactly," Montero said quickly. "It's simply a matter of finding the right person." He gave Alejandro a sly smile. "Do you know of such a man?"

Alejandro returned the smile. "There might be one at this banquet."

When Diego closed the door behind him he saw why the room was guarded. It was Montero's private study.

He looked up and caught his breath. On the wall behind Montero's desk hung a painting of Esperanza. For a moment he struggled to control his surging emotions. Then he tore his eyes away from the painting and scanned the room.

Against the far wall stood a chest banded with thick steel. Diego crossed the room and began trying the keys he'd taken from the guard.

Suddenly Diego heard the sound of approaching footsteps. They stopped outside the door.

Diego looked around and threw himself behind a large chair just as the door opened.

Don Luis entered. As Diego watched, the elderly aristocrat crossed to the steel-banded chest, unlocked it, and threw back the lid. Inside it were stacks of important-looking papers.

Diego saw Don Luis take a small, beautifully carved box out of the chest, then close the lid. A few moments after Don Luis left the room, Diego moved away from his hiding place and followed him.

As usual, Don Hector was boring everyone at the table with one of his political tirades.

"Santa Anna's lack of control has made the peasants headstrong," he rumbled, with a bulldog glare. "They imagine the return of Zorro in every stupid act of vandalism."

"Anyone can put on a mask and play Zorro," Love scoffed. "It requires only the price of the cloth."

Alejandro shrugged. "That's the problem, isn't it? It's difficult to kill a mask."

It annoyed Love to see Montero nodding agreement.

To the surprise of everyone, Elena spoke up. "Until these people are free to govern themselves, I think we'll see many more *Z*'s carved into walls," she said passionately.

Although Montero was extremely proud of his daughter, she could be quite headstrong at times. And this was one of those times. Not only was Elena discussing politics at the table with the men—something ladies did not do—she was defending Zorro's criminal actions!

Seeing her father's disapproving frown, Elena turned to Alejandro. "What do you think, Don Alejandro?"

"I think sheep will always need a shepherd," he said solemnly. Then he smiled. "But certainly not this Zorro creature. He probably wears the mask to hide his bald head and unsightly features."

Montero and his fellow noblemen laughed. But Alejandro was pleased to see Elena leap to Zorro's defense.

"There are some who would call him heroic," she said coldly.

Alejandro rolled his eyes. "Heroism. A romantic illusion."

"Much like nobility?" Elena demanded.

"Elena!" Montero said sharply.

Captain Love came to Elena's aid. "Heroism will always be the province of any man worth the name."

"Spoken like a true spear-carrier." Alejandro yawned. "All that playing with swords, firing guns, racing around on horses—it gives me a frightful headache." He nodded at Montero. "Such sweaty pursuits are hardly the work of a gentleman."

"And what is?" Elena snapped. "Climbing in and out of carriages?"

Alejandro gave her a small smile. "No, my dear. Increasing one's holdings so as to provide lavish comfort for young ladies like you."

Elena turned away in disgust. It annoyed her to think she had found this lazy young snob attractive. But Montero smiled and nodded his approval. Spoken like a true nobleman, he thought.

"Unfortunately," Alejandro went on, "our way of life is threatened by the lawlessness around us." He looked around the table. "I myself have been *this close* to some notorious bandits. Unless they are made to fear our strength, anarchy will prevail."

"I am sure they have much to fear from you, Don Alejandro," Elena said with obvious sarcasm.

"But he's right!" Don Peralta declared. "Why, only the other day I was robbed on a public street!"

Alejandro slapped the table in outrage. "Shocking! What kind of animal would do such a thing?"

"Maybe one who is hungry."

Elena's quiet voice silenced the table.

Alejandro looked at her. "Well," he said with a sigh, "I wouldn't know about hunger. But then again, neither would you."

Elena felt her face flush with anger.

Montero felt the tension and tried to lighten the mood. "A woman's grasp of politics," he joked. "What can I say?"

There was an uneasy silence around the table. Love seized the opportunity to get Elena off by herself. He stood up and bowed gracefully, determined not to be outdone by Alejandro's fine manners.

"We're at a party, aren't we? Elena, may I have the honor of this dance?"

Elena chose to end any unpleasantness. Acting the model daughter, she looked to Montero for his permission. Montero nodded grandly.

As Captain Love led Elena toward the dance area, Alejandro watched them with a calculating smile.

Love danced like a soldier, as if marching stiff-legged to the music. But that didn't stop Elena from flirting.

Elena draped a bare arm over Love's shoulder, then turned bright red when she saw Alejandro standing behind Love. The young aristocrat had a small smile on his face, as if he knew exactly the game she was playing.

Elena was both embarrassed and angry. "Yes?" she said sharply. "Are you looking for something?"

"A sense of the miraculous in everyday life," Alejandro said, his eyes locked on hers.

Love spun around, obviously annoyed. "Oh, really? Why don't you go look for it somewhere else? The lady and I were trying to dance."

"You were trying," Alejandro corrected. "She was succeeding."

Alejandro gave him an apologetic smile and put a friendly arm around his shoulder. "Forgive me, Captain Love. It was a shameless joke at your expense—and I hope it won't be the last. Don Rafael wants you back at his table."

Love blinked at him, slightly confused. With great reluctance he bowed to Elena and strode away.

Alejandro turned and opened his arms. Without a word Elena slipped into his embrace, and they began to dance. Although Elena did not approve of the polite young man, she had to admit he danced beautifully.

Diego also noticed how well they danced together. Too well, he thought.

Fresh from his little adventure in Montero's private study, Diego decided to remind his pupil why they were there. Just as he started to approach the couple, Diego noticed that all the guests were rising from their tables.

The moment Diego had warned Alejandro about had come. The aristocrats were preparing to gather privately. Something important—and highly secret—was about to take place.

Montero whispered something to Don Luis, and the two of them followed the others inside. Meanwhile

Alejandro was playing the fool with Montero's daughter.

As the music ended, Diego caught Alejandro's attention and jerked his head toward the departing guests.

Alejandro turned and got the message. He nodded to Diego as if to say, Don't worry, I'll be there with them.

Diego was surprised at how quickly Alejandro reacted. He turned to the bandleader and said something. Immediately the band launched into a wild and spirited tune.

Alejandro turned to Elena. "Would you care to try something more robust? Or maybe you're not up to the task."

Elena could not resist the challenge. "On the contrary, Don Alejandro. I think only of your distaste for perspiration." She smiled sweetly. "Shall we?"

The dance became more intense. The other dancers on the floor were fascinated. They gradually moved aside, clapping and cheering as Alejandro and Elena danced on.

Watching the way his young pupil was dancing, Diego smiled to himself and looked around for Montero. Sure enough, the powerful nobleman had stopped and was glaring at the two young dancers. Alejandro's little game was working like a charm.

As Montero watched the unladylike dancing, his outrage mounted. "Can you believe that girl?" he said to no one in particular. "Wild, just like her mother."

Diego saw Montero storm across the floor and yell something at the bandleader. Instantly the music ended. Reluctantly, Alejandro let Elena slip out of his arms.

Alejandro had seen Montero's reaction. In fact he had

been waiting for it. As Montero neared, Alejandro put on his most innocent face.

"Well!" Alejandro said to Elena, making sure Montero could hear. "If *that's* the way they're dancing in Madrid these days . . ."

Elena was taken completely unaware by his change in attitude. But the reason behind it became very clear when she saw her father coming.

"Don Rafael, excuse me. I need to catch my breath," Alejandro said, making a show of breathing heavily. "Your daughter is a very spirited dancer."

Suddenly the focus of Montero's anger shifted to Elena. " 'Spirited,' " Montero repeated. "Thank you for putting it so delicately."

Elena could not believe it. Alejandro had managed to put the entire blame on her. The cowardly fop had thrown her to the wolves to gain favor with her father. Elena fumed. Worst of all, her father was believing him.

"I apologize if you were offended," Montero said.

Unable to bear it, Elena shoved Alejandro aside and stormed off the floor.

Alejandro moved in for the kill. "Your apology is completely unnecessary, I assure you. She is young and impulsive, but her beauty is beyond compare," he observed. "And she has her father's commanding presence," Alejandro added. "As an adviser to Her Royal Highness in matters of finance, it would be my pleasure to introduce you both at court."

As always, Don Diego's advice was right on the mark. Montero bit hook, line, and sinker. He was a sucker for high society.

"Thank you, Don Alejandro," Montero said gratefully. "I would be honored."

This was going to be fun, Alejandro gloated.

Then Montero clapped a fatherly hand on Alejandro's shoulder. "Would you care to join us in the courtyard? There is something I want to share with you."

"What?" Alejandro asked innocently.

Montero leaned close. "A vision."

11

MONTERO GUIDED ALEJANDRO TO A PRIVATE COURT-yard lit by torches. In the middle of the courtyard was a huge wooden table. A shiny red Chinese box sat in the center.

The important guests were already seated around the great table. The others, like Alejandro, stood.

Montero walked over to a black curtain on the wall. "Fellow aristocrats of California," he said, addressing them with a smile. "All of us recall the golden years when we ruled this country. We were respected as noblemen. We grew wealthy. But we never determined our own destiny."

His smile faded. "The time has come—time to claim what should always have been ours. My friends, I give you the independent"—Montero pulled a cord, and the black curtain fell away—"Republic of California."

There were a few gasps when the guests saw the large

map of North America showing a whole new country: the country of California.

A few men applauded politely. Others frowned. Still others, like Alejandro, were fascinated. The elderly Don Peralta, one of the most respected of the landowners, stood up.

"Don Rafael, every man here owes you something. The land you gave us made us all wealthy," Don Peralta said, walking around the table. "But now you're asking us to raise arms against Santa Anna when you know we could never defeat his army."

"I'm not suggesting we fight him for California, my friend," Montero said. "I'm suggesting we buy it from him."

Over the murmurs of the assembled noblemen, Montero continued. "Santa Anna is fighting a war with the United States, and he is running out of money. I have already made a deal with him."

At this, Don Luis looked up. But Don Peralta wasn't finished.

"Even if we all combined our fortunes, we couldn't come up with enough money to buy California from Santa Anna." The old man turned away in disgust. "You're living in a dream."

Smiling, Montero moved to the table. "Very well," he said calmly. "Let us all live in the dream together."

With that he opened the red Chinese box. Inside was a beautiful bar of gold—so pure it seemed to glow against the velvet lining.

A hush fell over the guests. They stared in awe at the gleaming bar of gold.

Alejandro noticed that its smooth surface was stamped with the Spanish royal seal.

Montero savored the moment, smiling triumphantly at Peralta, before closing the box. Then he turned to his guests.

"Meet me here tomorrow for a trip that will open your eyes and lay all your doubts to rest."

As the excited guests filed past Montero to pay their respects, Alejandro knew every man would be there tomorrow. And so would Zorro.

It was a strange trip.

As Alejandro had predicted, all of the noblemen showed up early the next morning. They were seated in ornate coaches with black tarps over the windows to prevent them from seeing where Montero was taking them. Love's soldiers drove the coaches, while Love and Montero led the way on horseback.

Inside the stuffy coaches the guests were bumped and jostled by the rough trail. They were also sweating heavily from the morning sun. The long, secret journey was making them all irritated.

"He doesn't even trust us!" Don Peralta grumbled.

Don Hector shrugged. "Would *you* trust us?"

The other nobles laughed knowingly in the semidarkness. They had no illusions about their own corruption.

"It had better be worth it," Don Peralta muttered.

By the time the coaches arrived, everyone was cranky, uncomfortable, and sore. But the moment the travelers stepped into the sunlight their mumbling complaints stopped.

Spread out below them was a full-scale mining operation—gold mining.

It was like a small city. An elaborate network of

wooden platforms, water sluices, and train tracks led to tunnels inside the canyon walls.

Small ore carts ran on the tracks. They carried gold-bearing rocks from the mine tunnels. Once outside, the rocks were loaded into large metal buckets.

In the center of the entire operation, high on a platform, was a huge paddle wheel. The ore buckets were attached to the wheel by ropes. When the wheel turned, the buckets were hauled up to the platform.

A short distance from the crude elevators was the smelting house. There, using intense heat, the gold was separated from the rock.

Alejandro was both impressed and outraged. The water sluices, the rock piles, the mines—everything was worked by men in chains. Montero was using slave labor.

Alejandro spotted a familiar figure among the prisoners. It was Fray Felipe. The aged monk looked worn and sick. Women and children were also laboring as slaves. Alejandro realized this was what happened to all those who had disappeared. They'd been kidnapped by Love's soldiers.

Montero turned to the assembled guests and grandly gestured at the mine.

"This, gentlemen, is our Golden City, our El Dorado!"

Then he led them to a room cut into the canyon wall. At one end of the huge room was a steel cage. The cage was stacked high with gleaming metal bars. It looked like a mountain of pure gold.

Montero opened the cage. He chuckled, as if enjoying the moment immensely. "Technically, of course, all this gold belongs to Santa Anna." He winked at his friends. "Fortunately he is completely unaware of its existence."

He picked up a gold bar and showed it to his audience. "We have marked all of the bars with the Spanish seal, so Santa Anna will think they have come from Spain."

Montero's face glowed with triumph. "Do you see now, gentlemen?" he asked, smiling at Peralta.

Then the smile faded. "Two days from now we are going to buy this country from Santa Anna—with gold dug from his own land!"

The others laughed in admiration, enjoying Montero's clever plan. As an outlaw, Alejandro was also impressed. Montero was about to claim all of California as his private empire.

Alejandro thought of the starving women and children, enslaved to serve Montero's ambition. Perhaps Zorro could cut that ambition down to size.

The aristocrats buzzed excitedly as Love and Montero led them outside, into the glaring sunlight.

Kwoom! A sudden blast raised clouds of dust and sent sharp pieces of rock raining down on them. One side of the mountain crumbled like dirty brown snow. Panicked, the guests scurried back toward the gold room.

"Calm down, everyone!" Love barked. "It's all just part of the mining process. At first we were picking the gold off the ground. Now we're down to digging and blasting."

As Captain Love strutted like a tin soldier, Alejandro watched a young boy stagger under the heavy load strapped on his back. He recognized him as the boy who had sought refuge at the watering station. Obviously Love had caught up to him.

Alejandro smiled to cover his outrage. "So! This is the future of California!"

Montero nodded proudly. "Yes. This is my vision."

A madman's vision, Alejandro thought as he scanned the area.

Suddenly a loud cry turned his head. Alejandro glanced up and froze, eyes wide.

Sitting in one of the tiny train cars on the ridge was a wild man. He was whooping and waving a pickax.

The man had a grizzled beard, long, tangled hair, and three fingers on one hand. He was starved, dirty, and totally crazed, but Alejandro recognized his old sidekick, Three-Fingered Jack.

All activity in the area had stopped. Everyone was staring at Jack. Slowly he stood up in the tiny train car and opened his arms wide.

"Welcome, gentlemen," Jack croaked. "They call us the Disappeared Ones. But look around. As you can see, we haven't disappeared, we've just been a little hard to find."

Love stepped forward, shading his eyes against the bright sun. "You! I know you!"

"Of course you do. I'm the legendary Three-Fingered Jack!" He glared at the landowners and pointed his pickax. "And *you* are a bunch of murdering scum in fancy linen clothes."

Love clenched his jaw. "Ignore him, gentlemen. He's a common thief."

"Thief, yes—common, no!" Jack cried in mock outrage. "And I was nothing compared to you, gentlemen—nothing! I stole cash. I stole gold. But you—you steal people's lives!"

With terrifying speed Jack's rage exploded. *"Blood-sucking maggots!"*

Screaming at the top of his lungs, he kicked the hand brake off and sent the car hurtling toward the noblemen. *"Eeeaaghhh!"* Jack shrieked, waving the pickax.

Everyone scattered, except Love. Holding his ground as the train car careened closer, Love calmly lifted his rifle.

The car stopped with a jolt, catapulting Jack directly at Love, his pickax ready to strike.

Love stepped aside—and fired. The bullet struck Jack square in the heart. He hit the ground with a sickening thud.

A deep silence fell over the canyon. Everyone stared at the strange figure sprawled on the ground.

Instinctively Alejandro knelt beside the body and gently lifted Jack's head. For an instant their eyes met. Alejandro took his silk handkerchief and gently dabbed the blood from the corner of Jack's mouth.

Jack gave him a crooked smile. A moment later he was dead.

With great effort Alejandro put on a blank face as he stood up. He tucked the handkerchief back in his sleeve and shrugged at Love.

The captain studied Alejandro for a second. Then he swaggered closer and turned Jack over with the toe of his boot. As Love looked down at Jack's face he began to laugh softly.

Alejandro glared at him. "Something amusing, Captain?"

"Strange, I'd say, rather than amusing." Love was still staring at Jack. "That's the second time I've shot this man while he was flying through the air."

"Must be your passion for skeet shooting," Montero crowed. He moved off toward the coaches, followed by his guests. They were all laughing as if nothing had happened.

All around the canyon the guards were roughly urging the slaves back to work. Alejandro watched, bitter and brokenhearted. Abruptly he turned away and followed the others, struggling to control his cold fury.

Love's gaze remained fixed on Alejandro, his mind seething with suspicion. Then Love knelt beside the man he'd just killed. He pulled out a long bowie knife and placed it on Jack's wrist.

Later, when the noblemen were climbing back into their comfortable carriages, Alejandro heard someone call.

"Don Alejandro!"

He turned and saw Captain Love on horseback looking down at him. "I need to talk to you," Love barked. "Back at the stables. Alone."

Alejandro shrugged. "Perhaps some other time."

"Today," Love said sharply. "Alone." He wheeled his horse and trotted away.

Watching him go, Alejandro understood that Love had issued a challenge, not an invitation.

12

Diego enjoyed grooming Toronado. The stallion was so much like his own horse. He sang softly as he brushed the stallion's shining black coat.

Montero's stable seemed empty. Montero and his guests had ridden off. But someone was watching—and listening.

Elena had come in to get her horse. The sound of Diego's singing was charming. It also touched her in a way she couldn't quite understand, as if she'd heard the song in a dream.

Moving around to comb the stallion's mane, Diego saw Elena. The song faded from his lips, and his heart pounded.

Elena smiled, sorry she had interrupted his song. "Good afternoon, Bernardo," she said politely.

It pleased Diego that his noble daughter treated servants with dignity. It was the sign of a true lady.

"Senorita," he said hoarsely, then averted his eyes.

"Your voice is very calming," Elena told him. She moved closer to Toronado.

Diego wished she would go away. "The horse is high-spirited, senorita," he explained. "He needs to hear something soothing."

"Yes, I understand." She patted Toronado's neck. "How long have you worked for Don Alejandro?"

"Sometimes it seems like forever," Diego muttered.

Elena laughed, surprised.

Immediately, Diego realized his mistake. "I'm sorry. I speak out of place."

Elena put a finger to her lips. "Don't worry, Bernardo, he won't hear it from me." She leaned closer. "He's a very confusing man, Don Alejandro. Sometimes he puts on such airs, so arrogant, so superior. And yet the way he looks at me, the way he dances . . ." She smiled at Diego. "It's as if he's two completely different men." Elena picked up an extra brush and began to groom the horse, working beside Diego.

The emotions welling up at that moment were almost more than Diego could handle. "You look so much like your mother," he blurted out before he realized what he was saying.

Puzzled, Elena stopped and looked at him. "How would you know that?"

Good question, Diego thought as he dug for an answer. "I mean . . . you don't look anything like Don Rafael."

Elena laughed and continued brushing Toronado. "I know my father wishes I acted more like her. She was very proper, my mother. Always correct."

"Is that how he describes her?" Diego snorted.

"Yes. But sometimes I do not believe him."

Smart girl, Diego thought, hiding his smile. "Why not?" he asked. "Because you feel she was more like you?"

Elena shrugged. "Maybe I just want it to be so. It would be a way of knowing her." She lowered her voice as if telling a secret. "When I was young I used to sneak out through my window at night and ride my horse across the Spanish hills. My nanny told me the departed can see you in the moonlight. I waved at the sky so my mother would know it was me."

"You must have been something to see," Diego said softly. Their eyes met, and she smiled. "What happened to your mother?"

Elena's smile faded. "She died giving birth to me. Father rarely speaks of her. I think he finds it too painful."

The lying coward, Diego fumed, blaming Esperanza's death on Elena. Diego glanced up and saw her staring at him.

"Bernardo, I must ask you a question. Have we ever met before?"

The question made Diego wary. "Why do you say that?"

"I don't know. It's strange . . . your voice, it seems familiar somehow."

"But that's impossible," he said gently. "I haven't been to Spain . . . since before you were born."

Elena nodded and put down her brush. "Of course." Then she smiled. "Well, it's a very pleasant voice, anyhow."

"I'm glad you think so."

"Good day, Bernardo," she said, moving off.

"Good day, Elena," he said under his breath, watching her leave.

Diego stood there, overcome by the encounter with his long-lost daughter. Closing his eyes, he leaned his head against the stallion.

Alejandro accepted Love's challenge and arrived at the appointed hour. It comforted Alejandro to see that the barracks were still being repaired from his last visit.

Captain Love greeted Alejandro in his office and set out a pitcher of wine and two glasses. But as they sat across from each other, Alejandro saw Love fill his glass from a container under his desk.

The captain sat back and gave Alejandro a quizzical look, as if sizing him up.

"Did you know that the Jivaro Indians of South America eat their slain enemies in order to absorb their power? Seeing through the eyes of an enemy is a valuable thing."

Alejandro wondered if Love was trying to scare him. If so, it wasn't working. He adjusted his silk sleeve and waited.

Love sipped his drink, watching Alejandro intently. "And it's in a man's eyes that you can find the true measure of his soul." He took another sip and smiled.

"But where are my manners?" Love said tightly. "Would you care for a drink?"

Love reached down and suddenly brought up a large glass container and shoved it across the desk. It rotated as it slid toward Alejandro and stopped.

At first he saw a dark, murky shape floating inside the glass jar. But as Alejandro peered at the shape, it became horribly clear.

All the air left Alejandro's body as he stared at his brother's head. It took everything he had learned from Diego's intense training to keep his face blank.

Love shoved a smaller wine pitcher forward. "A different vintage perhaps?"

Jutting from the wine pitcher like a weird flower was a three-fingered hand—Three-Fingered Jack's.

Alejandro shrugged. "You're a very sick man, Captain Love."

"Heads in water, hands in wine pitchers . . . Such things must strike you as odd, I suppose," Love said scornfully.

"Well, for one thing I think you should fire your housekeeper." Alejandro nodded casually at Joaquin's head. "Who is he?"

"An enemy. He has a brother out there who will share the same fate." Love stared at him, making it clear whom he meant.

Unfazed, Alejandro smiled. "Well, I wish you luck." Eyes still locked on Love, Alejandro picked up a small silver cup, dipped it into the brine, and drank the salty liquid.

"To your health," Alejandro said coldly.

Love blinked. Then his eyes narrowed. "Murieta's brother or not, you are more than you pretend to be."

Alejandro dabbed his lips with a silk handkerchief. "Maybe someday I'll see what I look like through *your* eyes, Captain Love."

The veiled threat hung in the silence as Alejandro coolly got up and strolled outside.

Once outside, he hurried to a secluded alley behind the stables. There, concealed by a high fence, Alejandro pulled out his knife. With sudden fury he began stabbing a wooden bench, over and over again.

Tears streaming, Alejandro unleashed his rage the only way he could—for now. But Captain Love owed him for a brother and a friend.

Soon Zorro would come to collect.

Elena rode to the square, dismounted, and tied her horse to a hitching post. It was market day, and all the local farmers and artisans had set up stalls.

She moved slowly among the stalls, enjoying the bright array of fruit, flowers, tame birds, and Indian baskets and pottery.

An old woman tugged on Elena's skirt. Smiling, she pressed a yellow scarf into Elena's hand.

"It's beautiful," Elena said, slightly confused.

She didn't recognize the old woman as her childhood nanny, but Elena looked so much like her mother that the old woman knew her immediately. She said something in her native tongue and touched Elena's shoulder.

Elena tried the scarf on and was delighted. When she turned, the old woman was gone. Confused, Elena searched for the old woman and found her behind the stall, talking to a young Indian girl.

Elena smiled. "Excuse me. How much does this scarf cost?"

The Indian girl spoke to the old woman, who shook her head.

"It's a gift, she says," the girl explained. "In honor of your mother."

Elena gaped in disbelief. "My mother?"

"She loved your mother."

"Tell her she must be mistaken," Elena said, trying to regain her composure. "My mother died long ago, in Spain."

The Indian girl translated. The old woman made a dismissive gesture. She answered in a very no-nonsense manner, pointing at Elena's face.

"She says there is no mistaking the daughter of Diego and Esperanza de la Vega," the Indian girl said quietly. "She says she was your nanny. She hung flowers on your crib when you were little."

Heart racing and hands trembling, Elena held out the scarf. "Sorry. I cannot accept it."

The old woman waved a wrinkled hand and turned away. A moment later she disappeared behind another stall.

Too shaken to follow, Elena stood there, twisting the yellow scarf around her fist. It was the second time in two hours that a stranger had mentioned her mother.

Unable to forget the Indian woman's words, Elena got directions to the old de la Vega ranch.

She arrived near sunset and was taken by the spectacular view of the coastline. The rest of the estate was overgrown and choked with weeds.

As Elena moved through the charred ruins of the house, she turned and faced what had once been her nursery. Through the broken window she could see out to the horizon. She moved closer and noticed the flowers blooming just outside the window. They were part of a romania bush. Elena bent closer and took a deep breath.

The cool, sweet scent triggered a rush of memories and emotions. Suddenly she remembered a lullaby like the song Bernardo had been singing.

Battered by waves of unanswered questions, Elena made her way down to a wall overlooking the cove.

She sat there, watching the sun dip below the purple horizon, much the way her mother, Esperanza, had, twenty years before as she waited for Zorro to return home.

Alejandro was ready to explode.

Safely back at Diego's secret cave, he paced up and down, trying to walk off the anger and frustration.

Diego watched him carefully. At least his pupil had had the sense to come here. But from experience he knew that rage could erase all reason.

At the moment Alejandro was muttering under his breath. A bad sign.

"Listen to me," Diego said quietly.

No answer.

"Listen to me!" Diego shouted.

Alejandro stopped pacing and looked at him.

"You must go to Montero's house *tonight,"* Diego said firmly. "Break into the chest in his study. Look for anything that will tell us where the mine is."

Alejandro shook his head. "I'll see that jar for the rest of my life."

Diego's tone went from firm to hard. "Your brother is dead, Alejandro! You must put it aside!"

But Diego understood what it was like to lose someone, to burn for revenge. "We lose the ones we love," he said softly. "We cannot change that. Alejandro, listen to me. You are ready."

He clapped a hand on Alejandro's shoulder.

"It is time for Zorro to return."

The moment Alejandro had dreamed of since childhood had finally arrived—the moment of becoming Zorro. But it was marked with cruel irony.

"I do not feel ready," he said quietly. "People are

dying at the mine, and all I can think of is Captain Love."

Diego nodded in sympathy. "You will have your chance. He will come into your circle soon enough. You need not chase him."

"How? How can I do what is needed when all I feel is hate?"

In answer Diego produced the black mask of Zorro. "With this."

He lifted the mask and tied it around Alejandro's head. It was a grant of power—like an angel getting his wings.

The little ritual had a tremendous impact on Alejandro. Immediately he felt a weight being lifted from his spirit.

"Thank you, Don Diego," he said, voice hushed.

Diego squeezed his shoulder. "You've earned it."

He went to the wall and took his sword. "Now we must ride to Montero's place. You will go over the wall at my signal."

"What is the signal?"

Diego's eyes gleamed in the torchlight.

"You will know."

13

RAFAEL MONTERO WAS EXTREMELY TENSE.

In twenty-four hours California would belong to him. He chewed nervously on his fine cigar as he sat in his private courtyard with Captain Love.

Spread out before them on the table was a detailed map of the gold mine.

Love savored the expensive cigar Montero had given him. He had a taste for wealth and a hunger for power. Montero could give him both.

"Think of it," Love murmured. "By this time tomorrow night you'll own every mountain and beach in all California."

The news seemed to make Montero more nervous. "Unless . . ."

"What?"

Montero chewed his cigar. "Unless Santa Anna somehow finds out about the mine."

Love pondered the problem. He came up with a crude

solution. "Then we'll have to destroy the evidence—bury the mine completely."

"Impossible," Montero objected. "How do you plan to set the explosives and get all the workers out by noon?"

"I don't," Love said evenly.

Montero stared, not sure he had heard correctly.

"We destroy *all* the evidence. No witnesses."

A deadly quiet followed Love's words.

Montero was about to strongly object when—

"Fire! *Fire!*"

Alarmed by the cry, Montero and Love raced inside. Montero led the way to the kitchen. They burst through the door, past boiling pots and women cooking, and rushed to the window.

As Montero threw back the shutters, his face was lit by a crimson glow. Love peered through the window.

There across the valley was a huge blazing *Z* of flames. It illuminated the entire hillside.

Montero's face went ghostly white in the dancing firelight.

"It's happening again," he whispered.

Across the valley, Diego wheeled his horse, knowing that Montero—and Zorro—had seen his signal.

As expected, Montero's men rode off across the valley in pursuit of Zorro. But Zorro was right there, unseen, waiting for them to leave. As the soldiers galloped past the courtyard, Zorro appeared on top of the wall.

He jumped onto a nearby balcony overlooking the courtyard. Quickly he moved toward a door at the far end, then paused.

On the table below were a number of documents. Zorro hopped over the railing and lightly dropped down to the ground floor.

Zorro couldn't believe his good fortune.

One of the documents was a map of the gold mine. He heard footsteps inside. Instantly Zorro sprang upward and clung to a balcony pillar. A second later Montero strode into the courtyard and headed to the table.

About ten feet above him, clinging to the top of the pillar, Zorro watched Montero scoop up the map.

As he adjusted his grip on the pillar, Zorro dislodged a large potted plant. It teetered like a tenpin, then fell—directly toward Montero's table.

Zorro snatched the plant. The impact almost separated the plant from the heavy pot—but it held.

Below him, Montero paused as if sensing an intruder. Then he shook his head and left the courtyard, passing right under Zorro. Seconds after he disappeared into the house, the plant gave way and the pot shattered on the courtyard tiles below.

A moment later Zorro dropped to the ground and followed Montero inside.

The hallway was deserted. Cautiously Zorro went upstairs and peeked around the corner. There was no sign of Montero. Moving down the hall, he saw an open door. Inside was Montero's study.

The room was empty. But on the wall hung a large oil painting of a woman. She looked remarkably like Elena.

Curious, Zorro stepped closer. Suddenly he heard footsteps approaching. He looked around wildly for someplace to hide. But there was nothing that could conceal him.

Just outside the open door, Montero paused, visibly shaken.

"Did you send men to the hills?" he asked Love. "Double the guards at the wall?"

Captain Love hid his annoyance behind an obedient bow. "Yes, yes, of course," he assured Montero. But Montero had him worried.

As they entered the study, Love tried to calm Montero down. "After all, if we're looking for only one man, then—"

Montero slammed the map and papers down on the desk. "It's not one man. It's Zorro!" He turned and walked to the window. "And he knows about the mine. Otherwise he wouldn't be here tonight."

"How could he possibly—"

As Love asked the question, a silver sword came down from above. Unseen by the two men, the sword's tip gently dropped toward the map on Montero's desk.

"It doesn't matter how!" Montero snapped. "If Santa Anna learns we've paid him with his own gold, we're finished."

Right above them, spread over the rafters like a black bat, Zorro took it all in. He thrust his arm down and speared the map. Silently, he lifted the map like a hooked fish.

Montero picked up the papers from his desk and handed them to Love.

"Make sure these papers are somewhere safe," he murmured. "I have to speak to my Elena."

Love took the papers and watched Montero leave.

Above him, Zorro unhooked the map from the tip of his sword. He waited a few seconds after Love departed, then swung lightly down to the floor.

Quickly he peered out the window.

There were guards everywhere.

Love was halfway down the hall, sorting Montero's papers, when he realized the map was gone.

He stopped and shuffled through the papers once again. No map.

Love glanced back at the study. "Guards!" he shouted.

Drawing his sword, Love ran back toward the study door. As his hand touched the knob, the door suddenly swung open.

On the other side stood a man wearing a black mask. They gaped at each other, face-to-face.

Before Love could say "Zorro," a cold blade dug into his throat.

"Do as I say," Zorro warned, "or your mother will lose a son."

He pushed Love against the wall and took his sword. Love tried to resist, but Zorro's blade jabbed his neck hard.

Unarmed, Love allowed himself to be forced backward along the hall. Zorro's sword was still jammed against his throat when they turned the corner.

Zorro stopped. Directly ahead were two guards with muskets. They raised their weapons to fire.

Fortunately Captain Love made an excellent shield. The guards couldn't get a clear shot.

"Put down your weapons and come this way," Zorro said calmly. "Your captain is not bulletproof."

The guards hesitated. Zorro gave Love a little jab. "Tell them!"

"Do as he says!" Love rasped.

The guards dropped their weapons and moved closer to Zorro and Love.

"Stop," Zorro ordered.

The guards stopped. Uncertainly they stood next to a large bay window overlooking the courtyard.

"Turn and face the window."

The guards turned. Zorro pressed his blade into Love's neck, moving him forward until they were behind the guards.

"Bend over. Touch your toes," Zorro told the guards. "I know it's hard in a uniform."

Again the guards hesitated. They glanced at each other as if dealing with a madman.

Zorro jabbed Love, who grunted in pain.

"Do it!"

Zorro was right. It *was* hard to bend over in a uniform. The guards' pants seemed about to split.

Without removing the blade from Love's throat, Zorro turned and delivered two sharp kicks. His boot sent both guards rocketing through the window in a shower of glass. They tumbled into the courtyard below.

In another wing of the house, Montero heard the sound and threw open a window. He glanced down at the two fallen soldiers. Then he saw Elena watching from the doorway and his anger flared.

At all costs Elena had to be protected from Zorro.

Zorro was moving fast, prodding Love along the long hall. They stepped over the muskets dropped by the two guards and stopped.

"Turn around," Zorro barked.

Love turned, certain he was about to be stabbed in the back.

Instead, Zorro put his sword in his belt and scooped up the guns. At the same moment he glimpsed movement reflected in a mirror in front of him. Three guards were coming up behind him. Without hesitation Zorro flipped the muskets over his shoulders and fired backward!

The first two guards staggered back, firing wildly into the ceiling. Their bullets shattered the chandelier, which came crashing down on the third guard. Seizing the moment, Love whirled and body-slammed Zorro to the floor.

Dazed, Zorro saw Love race to one of the fallen guards and snatch his sword.

When Love turned, Zorro was already up and ready.

From the first clash of swords both men knew they'd need all their skill to survive. Love's anger surged through his muscles, and his strong strokes drove Zorro back.

Their blades moved at dazzling speed as Zorro countered with a deadly flurry that kept Love busy. Suddenly Love spun and backhanded Zorro against the wall.

Zorro blinked, trying to focus. Love moved in to strike.

At that moment Montero rounded the corner.

When he saw the black specter of Zorro looming up from the past, Montero almost fainted.

Horrified, he watched Zorro push away from the wall and attack Love. Zorro's brilliant series of thrusts and parries drove Love back.

With a roar Montero drew his sword and joined the battle. Ghost or human, he'd kill Zorro.

Suddenly Zorro had Montero attacking on his right and Love on his left. He drew the sword he had taken from Love. With a weapon in each hand Zorro fought them both at the same time!

But despite his skill, the odds were too great. In a few seconds one blade or another would end Zorro's brief career. Montero slashed, Love thrust . . . and Zorro threw himself backward through an open door—landing in a darkened room.

Montero and Love charged inside after him.

Only vague shapes could be seen in the darkness, but the three men battled furiously. Swords hissing, they slashed at the dancing shadows.

Then Love found himself fighting Zorro alone. With a series of brilliant strokes Love sent him crashing to the floor. Zorro was helpless.

Now it was Love's turn. He pressed his blade hard into his hated enemy's throat.

14

"GUARDS!" LOVE CRIED TRIUMPHANTLY.

Instantly three soldiers arrived, one carrying a torch. Laughing wildly, Love snatched the torch.

"So!" he crowed. "The great Zorro meets his master!"

Flourishing the torch, he let the light splash over the prisoner on the floor. Love's face sagged.

It was Montero!

"You idiot!" Montero sputtered. "You stupid fool! You let him escape!"

Zorro crouched on the long balcony overlooking the courtyard. He was retracing his earlier steps to make his escape. Below him he saw five men rush into the courtyard, led by Sergeant Garcia.

Footsteps clattered behind him as a group of soldiers ran through the house, toward the balcony.

Zorro pressed himself against the wall, glancing left and right for a way out. But he didn't see the dark figure standing in the shadows, watching his every move.

Half hidden by a curtain, Elena saw the masked bandit sprint away as the guards burst onto the balcony.

Elena's emotions wavered from loyalty to her father to fear for Zorro—especially when Zorro's escape was blocked by a squad of soldiers coming up the stairs to the balcony.

Suddenly Zorro stood trapped between two groups of guards. Swords raised, both groups charged, yelling like madmen.

"Excuse me, gentlemen," Zorro muttered. "I'm going to step out for some air."

Nimbly he plunged headfirst over the rail into the courtyard below. The charging guards collided in a tangle of fallen bodies and angry shouts.

Catlike, Zorro landed on his feet, only to find Sergeant Garcia waiting with his men. They attacked, backing Zorro up against the big table.

One reckless soldier rushed in wildly.

Zorro merely sidestepped, whacking the man's head as he went sprawling. Then he spun around and used the man's back as a ladder as he ran up onto the table.

"Ah, what a beautiful night to run someone through," Zorro said, whipping his blade with dazzling speed. "Who would like to be first?"

From his perch Zorro was able to hold off the remaining guards for a moment while he looked for a way out of the courtyard. The only escape route seemed to be upward. Zorro jumped and grabbed a tree branch that overhung the table.

Hanging on with one hand, he swung his sword with the other when Montero and Love burst into the courtyard. Realizing that they were more expert swordsmen than the clumsy guards, Zorro made his move.

He clenched his sword in his teeth, grabbed the overhanging branch with both hands, then flew over the heads of his attackers. As they turned, Zorro ran to a giant canvas map of California that hung on the wall.

Sword ready, he faced his enemies. Montero and Love led the charge. At the last possible moment Zorro slashed the ropes that held the large map. The huge square of canvas billowed like a sail and crashed down on the attackers.

Zorro vaulted over the writhing canvas. When the soldiers finally scrambled after him, he had vanished.

At dawn the entire platoon was still out looking for Zorro.

As the first rays of the sun crept over the estate's outer wall, four mounted soldiers galloped past Montero's stable.

A shadowy form rose up from behind the water trough. The figure ran to the stable door.

Zorro dashed inside. A few of the horses whinnied nervously. He slouched against the wall, waiting for them to settle down.

The door behind him slammed shut.

Zorro whirled. Elena was standing there, dressed in a robe. In her right hand was a sword.

As their eyes met, a pair of guards ran past the stables, shouting something.

"Good morning, senorita," Zorro said calmly.

Elena smiled. "Good morning, senor."

"You should be more careful," he warned, returning her smile. "There are dangerous men about."

Elena's smile faded. She held out her hand.

"Give it to me," she said sharply.

"What?"

"Whatever it is you stole from my father—I want it back."

Zorro laughed and headed for the door. As he started to move past her, Elena leveled her sword.

"Oh, come now," Zorro groaned. As he continued toward the door, Elena lunged. Her thrust was fast, accurate—and deadly.

Zorro ducked and drew his own sword. Rather than fight her, he leaped aside. "I don't have time to give you the proper instruction."

Elena cut off his escape. "I've had the proper instruction since I was four."

She lunged. Her blade cut Zorro's shirt.

Zorro fingered the cut. Then he saluted her—and attacked. Their steel blades flickered like lightning. They moved quickly back and forth. Slowed down by her robe, Elena shrugged it off and fought in her nightgown.

Zorro's blade sliced the gown, exposing one shoulder.

"Not bad," she congratulated him.

"Not bad at all," Zorro agreed, returning the compliment.

Elena moved in again. This time Zorro sliced the other shoulder of her gown. "You're not catching the strong of the blade," he told her.

His mocking words stoked Elena's anger. She snatched up her robe and used it like a cape. She snapped the robe in his face to distract him, then struck.

Elena's blade sliced his shirt from chest to shoulder.

"Ah, quite impressive," Zorro complimented her.

"Indeed!" Elena replied, noticing Zorro's corded muscles.

Confident now, Elena moved in, sword hissing like a snake. She caught Zorro's blade in her robe and twisted. The sword flew from his hand and went clattering across the room.

"This will make my task more difficult," Zorro admitted with a rueful smile.

Elena grinned triumphantly—and charged.

Zorro tumbled backward into a bale of hay. As he rolled, Elena slashed at him.

With perfect timing Zorro clicked his heels together. Sparks flew as his spurs clamped Elena's blade and yanked it from her hand.

Unarmed, Elena ran to pick up Zorro's fallen sword. As he leaped to his feet, he weighed her sword in his hand. It was much lighter than his. That meant Elena would be slower and he'd be much faster.

Sure enough, his brilliant sword strokes had Elena barely defending herself. Suddenly Zorro lunged. His blade snapped the sword from her hand. It flew into the wall and stuck.

"You fought bravely," he said, sighing. "But in the end you were undone."

She stared at him intently, eyes shining.

Zorro gently put the point of his sword against her neck and moved her back. Elena leaned against a bale of hay, her face lit by golden sunlight pouring through a high window. She looked beautiful.

"Do you surrender?" he asked softly.

"Never," she whispered. "But I may scream."

"I sometimes have that effect."

He kissed her. Then he lifted his head and stared into her eyes. Elena did not resist as he bent closer again.

But this time he didn't kiss her. He picked up his hat, put it on, and touched the brim.

"Good day, senorita."

Zorro tossed her sword so that it stuck in a pillar and pulled his own blade from the wall. Sword in hand, he leaped onto a ladder, then climbed to the loft.

A moment later he vanished.

As Elena breathlessly watched him go, she felt a twinge of disappointment.

Suddenly the doors flew open. Montero rushed into the stable, followed by Love, Garcia, and some guards.

"Elena!" Montero gasped, seeing her torn nightgown. "What are you doing here? What happened?"

Elena looked at him dazedly. "Zorro . . . Zorro was here. I fought him. Then he left." A flash of anger reddened her face. "He *left!*"

Montero rushed back to the open door. The area was deserted. Elena pulled her sword from the pillar, still thinking about Zorro's kiss.

"Could you tell who he was?" her father asked. "Did you recognize him?"

Elena tried to regain her composure. "No, but he was young and . . . vigorous. *Extremely* vigorous."

To Montero's surprise she angrily slashed the air with her sword. Somewhat puzzled, he studied his daughter. Whatever was wrong with her, he didn't like it.

The sound of hoofbeats outside drew Montero's attention. He followed Love to the door, closely trailed by Garcia.

"No sign of anyone, sir," the soldier reported to Love. "We covered the area east of—"

"All right," Love snapped. "Go to the bridge, cut off his retreat."

"Yes, sir."

As they galloped off, Love turned to Garcia. "Take your men, search the woods. If you find him, kill him. If you're not sure it's him—kill him anyway."

But even Love's deadly orders failed to ease Montero's rage. Eyes burning with hatred, Montero moved closer to Love.

"This had better be the end of it," he said through clenched teeth.

Horses' hooves crashed through the silent forest. Garcia and his mounted guards weaved their way through the trees, determined to hunt down their prey.

"Spread out!" Garcia yelled. "Give him no openings."

As the mounted soldiers formed a line, Zorro peered from the undergrowth. He waited until the soldiers disappeared into the trees beyond, then stepped into view.

Zorro let out a shrill whistle. A black stallion thundered out of the trees toward him.

Some distance away, Garcia heard the whistle. He reined his horse and shouted, "I hear him—this way!"

The guards wheeled and galloped back in Zorro's direction. Hearing the approaching troops, Zorro ran toward Toronado. He grabbed the saddle.

"Time to show you're more than just handsome. Let's be off!"

Zorro spoke too soon. On the word "off," Toronado took off. But Zorro wasn't quite in the saddle. Toronado dragged him, yelling, through the thick underbrush.

Finally Zorro tumbled and found himself lying next to a fallen tree.

He started to get up, then ducked behind the tree as Garcia and his men galloped past, after Toronado.

As the last soldier in the line rode past, Zorro jumped to his feet. He hopped onto the tree and sprinted along the trunk until he caught up to the last rider.

Zorro leaped and landed on the horse, right behind the saddle and rider.

"Excuse me—is this seat occupied?"

As the guard turned, Zorro knocked him to the ground and rode off.

The military single-file formation Garcia had ordered suited Zorro perfectly. He rode up close to the last guard in line, jumped onto his horse, and smacked the rider off.

One after another Zorro unseated the guards, working his way up the file until only Garcia remained.

Zorro decided to give Garcia a special send-off.

Totally unaware of what had happened behind him, Garcia charged after Zorro's black stallion. When he delivered the masked bandit's body to Montero he would be a rich man, Garcia gloated.

Suddenly a dark thundercloud passed over his head. Garcia looked up and his eyes bulged out.

Swooping over him, cape billowing like black wings, was Zorro!

Standing circus-style on two horses, Zorro galloped right over Sergeant Garcia.

Dead ahead and coming fast was a low-hanging tree branch.

Zorro blocked Garcia's view—until the instant he jumped over the branch.

Zorro landed on the speeding pair of horses and kept going. Garcia wasn't so lucky.

The plump sergeant barely saw the thick branch before it walloped him. *Phhwackk!* Garcia flew backward and landed in a stunned heap.

Still standing on the two horses, Zorro caught up to Toronado and leaped. He dropped into the silver saddle, gave Toronado the spur—and raced off to freedom.

15

SAFELY BACK IN THE SECRET CAVE, ALEJANDRO proudly showed Diego the map to Montero's gold mine.

The young Zorro's blood was still tingling from his adventures. "Here," he said, pointing to the map. "This is the canyon. That is where the mine is. They have twenty-five or thirty guards at most—nothing that Zorro can't overcome," he added, grinning at Diego. "Or *two* Zorros for that matter."

Diego turned away. "I'm not going with you," he said quietly.

"What?"

Diego's eyes blazed in the torchlight.

"There is something I must do. A personal matter."

For a moment Alejandro couldn't speak. When he did, his voice betrayed his shock—and anger. "Another one of your secrets? What about the prisoners?"

"There is nothing more I can do for them."

"You mean nothing you *will* do," Alejandro said

contemptuously. "You ignore their suffering. You think only of yourself."

"I gave my life to them!" Diego roared. Then his anger trailed off into pain. "You know what being Zorro did for me?" he muttered, almost to himself. "I lost everything."

His harsh whisper stabbed the quiet like barbed wire. "My wife was murdered before my eyes. My child stolen to be raised by my worst enemy."

Diego lowered his head. His sorrow filled the silence.

But Alejandro heard something else. "Elena . . . she's your daughter," he said softly.

"She *was.*"

"So you will simply take your revenge."

Diego's head jerked up. "I will take my daughter," he rasped, his face pale with rage. "And don't pretend she means nothing to you."

Alejandro didn't deny it. But he had lost everything, too. Anger flooded his voice. "You taught me to see beyond personal feelings. Was that all a lie?"

"You are too young to understand."

"To understand what? Betrayal?" Alejandro demanded, his jaw knotted with fury. "All the work, all the training, all the wise words—for what? To smile in the face of my brother's killer while you make your own plans?"

"No, Alejandro." Diego sighed. "I taught you what you needed to survive. But now I must look to my own heart."

He glanced defiantly at Alejandro. "She's all I have left. I am not going to lose her again."

Meanwhile my brother is still dead, Alejandro

thought bitterly. "And what about California?" he demanded. "What about the people?"

Diego shrugged. "They still have Zorro."

Alejandro gave Diego a final look of contempt, then turned and marched out of the cave.

On his way he passed the wooden table where Diego kept his gold cross and candles. With a vicious swat Alejandro knocked over the shrine and kept going.

Harrison Love's buckskin horse was foaming with sweat as he raced at full gallop into Rafael Montero's ranch. The guards stepped back to let their captain through.

Love found Montero sitting in the courtyard. The powerful Spaniard was gazing fixedly at the large map of California on the wall, the same map Zorro had cut down earlier that day.

Montero's face looked odd, as if he was gripped by some hallucination. Love cautiously moved to the table.

"I've got every inch of the courtyard covered," Love said crisply. "If he shows himself . . ."

Suddenly he realized Montero wasn't listening. "Are you all right?"

Montero rolled his eyes toward Love. "Do you have the map?"

"We'll find it," Love assured him.

Montero wasn't convinced. "Is your army ready to fight Santa Anna's troops?"

"No, sir," Love said slowly.

"Then why are you asking me if I'm all right? *Of course I'm not all right!"* Montero's voice turned cold.

"I'm starting to wonder whether you want this operation to succeed, Captain Love."

Love did not take the accusation lightly. He slammed his hand on the table. "What are you saying, Don Rafael?"

"I'm saying my horse could run this army better than you."

For a long moment the two men glared at each other, on the brink of a duel. Love's hand hovered over his pistol.

But his military training reined in his temper. Montero was his commander and his employer, as well as Elena's father. "I said I'll find him," Love said coldly. "That means I will."

"Maybe I can save you the trouble."

At the sound of the new voice Montero felt cold steel against his throat. He looked down and saw a sword extending from a shadowy archway.

Instantly Love went for his pistol.

"Go ahead," the voice said calmly. "Reach for it, Captain."

Hearing the deadly threat in the man's tone, Love slowly lowered his hand.

Fear rippled across Montero's skin. "Who are you?"

"I warned you, Rafael, that you would never be rid of me," the voice replied from the shadows.

The sword slowly slid down Montero's neck, pulling aside his collar. Underneath it was the old *Z* scar.

All color drained from Montero's face. "De la Vega . . ."

Diego stepped out of the darkness. "Hello, Rafael."

Montero peered at him. "You . . . you were not the

Zorro I saw last night." Then the truth dawned on him. He smiled ruefully at Diego. "It was your 'master,' Don Alejandro."

Diego's face revealed nothing. "There are many who would gladly wear the mask."

Totally confused, Love gaped at Diego.

"Either way, you're too late." Montero's smile became a nasty scowl. "Events have been set in motion that you cannot stop."

"I'm not here to stop you," Diego corrected. He pressed his sword against Montero's throat. "Call for Elena."

Montero glared at him, eyes bright with hatred.

"Call for her, Rafael, or you will never call for anything else again."

Diego pressed the sword deeper, the steel tip almost drawing blood. Realizing Diego would kill him, Montero gestured at Love.

"Bring my daughter here, Captain."

"Sir?" Love said, unable to believe Montero would endanger Elena.

"Bring her!"

Love backed away, not knowing if Montero was a coward or a genius.

Finally alone, the two old enemies stood face-to-face. "You can't imagine how many different ways I've dreamed of killing you, Rafael," Diego said quietly. "I've imagined tortures that would sicken even you."

"Really?" Montero murmured. "I've never given *you* a second thought."

Diego laughed. He grudgingly admired Montero's

defiant pose. However, he could see Montero's hand shaking.

But Montero also had a weapon. "Do what you will, de la Vega. If I die, the truth dies with me."

For a moment Diego seemed uncertain.

"Father!"

Both men turned and saw Elena run into the courtyard, Love close behind her. For an instant Diego thought she had called him. Then he saw her eyes and realized that all she saw was the servant Bernardo holding a sword at her father's throat.

"Bernardo! What are you doing?"

Diego could stand it no longer. "Tell her, Rafael," he warned.

Sensing his advantage, Montero said nothing.

"Tell me what?" Elena demanded. "What's going on?"

"Tell her who her real father is!" Diego cried, pushing his blade harder. A trickle of blood ran down Montero's neck. For a moment he wavered.

Then Montero smiled. "This very unfortunate man lost a daughter once, and it has driven him mad," he explained calmly. "Now he seeks to claim you for his own."

Diego's frustration mounted. If he killed Montero, Elena would never know the truth.

"Tell her how her mother died."

"Your daughter is gone, de la Vega. You can't have mine," Montero said with a trace of mockery.

"De la Vega?"

Elena's question rang through the quiet like a church bell.

Montero realized he'd made a mistake. As he turned to face Elena, Love kept his eyes on Diego, waiting for a chance to kill him.

Torn between confusion and shock, Elena tried to explain. "A woman in town . . . she told me about . . ." Elena looked at Diego. *"Diego* de la Vega?"

Diego nodded, heart swelling with emotion.

Elena glanced back at Montero. "Father?"

Montero hesitated. "His name is of no consequence," he said finally.

Unconvinced, Elena turned again to Diego. "I was told my nanny used to hang something on my crib."

Heady with elation, Diego turned to answer. "Yes. Your mother had her put fresh—"

Before Diego could finish the sentence, Love pounced. Without hesitating, he drew his pistol and aimed at Diego.

"No!" Elena threw herself in front of Diego, trying to shield him.

For a horrifying moment both Diego and Montero relived the night Esperanza died. And both moved at the same time.

Desperately Montero smacked Love's arm aside as Diego pushed Elena out of harm's way.

Love's shot went wild.

At the sound of his pistol three guards came running into the courtyard. They stopped, rifles leveled on Diego. Again Elena moved in front of Diego.

"No!"

But Diego refused to use his daughter for a shield. He stepped into the open, sword raised and ready to fight.

"Drop your sword," Montero said wearily, "or I will have no choice but to have you shot." He nodded at Elena. "Even in the presence of my daughter."

Despite his casual manner, Elena could tell he meant it. She also realized she couldn't expect him simply to set Diego free. She looked at Diego pleadingly.

"Please, Diego. Give up your sword."

Diego's eyes met hers, and he felt her fear. Slowly he let the sword slip out of his hand. As the blade hit the floor, two guards rushed to grab his arms while the third covered them.

Before they could hustle him away, Diego turned to Elena. "Flowers," he said quietly. "Romania."

Elena's face went pale. A rush of emotions tumbled through her thoughts. Elena remembered the woman in the market and the sweet childhood scent of romania when she arrived on the beach. Unable to speak, she watched the soldiers haul Diego out.

As Diego was led past Montero he jerked to a stop. His face was inches from Montero's.

"She knows," Diego whispered.

Montero smiled. "You're dead," he whispered back. Montero's smile became a nasty scowl as he leaned closer to Diego. "I would love to kill you now and put your suffering to rest. But I must kill Zorro, and only you know where he is. For that you will live a few more hours."

Montero gestured at the guards. "Lock him up."

As they dragged Diego away, Montero moved across the room and embraced Elena. "Thank heaven," he murmured. "You could have been killed."

Elena gently pulled back from his embrace. "I want to know the truth," she said firmly.

Montero's expression became hard. "I told you the truth: the man is insane."

"I want you to answer me," Elena insisted. "Is Diego my father?"

The question echoed in the sudden silence.

Montero heaved an impatient sigh. "I am your father and always will be. Now go inside."

For a long moment Elena studied him, as if the truth might be etched in his stony features. Finally, aware that he would say nothing more, Elena turned and hurried into the house.

When she was gone, Montero wheeled on Love.

"If you ever, *ever* endanger my daughter again, I will kill you," Montero said with cold fury.

Love stood his ground. "And if he had told her the truth?" he asked quietly.

Unable to answer, Montero moved toward the stairs. "Call for the horses. We are riding to the mine."

As the two men left, a shadowy figure emerged from an alcove. Elena had heard everything.

Her eyes flashed like black lightning as she realized what she had to do.

Like someone trapped in a recurring nightmare, Diego was hurled onto the stone floor of a dungeon.

He lay there until the guards were gone, then slowly got to his feet.

The first thing he did was check the door hinges. Unfortunately they were solid. He tried but couldn't budge the pins holding them.

Diego was still examining the door when he heard footsteps. He jumped back as a key turned the lock.

The door opened and the guard stepped inside.

The guard had an odd look on his face.

There was a sudden flash of movement and a pistol butt whacked the guard's head.

As the guard crumpled to the floor, Diego saw Elena standing there, pistol in hand.

16

THE SUN GLINTED OFF LOVE'S TELESCOPE AS HE CAREfully scanned the mine area for any sign of Zorro.

There was none. The slaves moving along the network of wooden bridges and train tracks were all working as usual. Love lowered the telescope. He handed it to Montero, who was crouched beside him on the ridge.

"We're here ahead of him," Love said with some relief. "He's nowhere to be seen."

Montero scanned the mine, then took a long drink from his canteen. "No reason for celebration," he muttered. "There are still two hours left."

The two men mounted their horses and began moving down the steep trail to the mine.

Below them the guards were overseeing the transfer of the gold. They watched closely as slaves passed the heavy ingots from hand to hand. Then the gold was loaded into an elevator basket. Slaves on the platform above turned the large paddle wheel, pulling up the baskets.

Finally the baskets were hauled up and the ingots stacked onto a waiting wagon.

When Love arrived, he immediately went down to the mine in search of Zorro. Montero stood on a platform, watching the entire operation.

The work seemed to be going slowly. Montero looked down impatiently, then walked over to the loaded wagon. He pulled the cover back and gazed at the neat stacks of gold piled inside. The wagon carried a king's ransom.

In two hours he would be king, Montero gloated. Ruler of all California.

Below him soldiers were carrying powder kegs into the four main mine shafts. Other guards were unrolling long fuses out of each tunnel.

Seeing their preparations, two young slave boys glanced at each other in terror, understanding that the mine was going to be blown up—as well as the slaves. A soldier pushed the boys toward the tunnel exit with his rifle.

Inside one of the shafts, an older slave dropped to the ground from exhaustion. A guard tried to shake him awake, to no avail.

"Water!" the guard shouted down the tunnel.

A hooded monk emerged from the shadows with a water pail. He bent down to ladle water into the slave's mouth. As the slave's eyes opened, he saw the black mask inside the monk's hood.

Zorro put a finger to his lips.

Outside, the four long fuses were being bound together into one. Everything was set for the final blast.

Love waved to the chief guard. "All right," he shouted. "Lock them up."

The guards began herding the slaves into large cages at the base of the canyon. Terrified, slaves stumbled down ladders and scaffolds, falling over in their panic.

Each shaft was checked for stragglers. As the last guard left one tunnel, he noticed something on the ground. It was a discarded monk's robe. Puzzled, the guard moved back inside. Instantly he was knocked out cold.

Zorro, wearing his familiar black cloak and mask, hurried toward the tunnel exit. Once outside, he took cover behind an ore cart.

Below him, Zorro could see the last prisoners being shoved into huge cages. He looked the other way and saw gold ingots being loaded onto the bucket elevator.

Love was supervising the loading. When the last ingot was placed, the guards pushed the slave out of the elevator. The slave was then escorted to a cage.

As the bucket rose to the top of the platform the slaves began pushing against the bars of their cages.

Montero checked his watch. It read ten minutes before eleven. He waved a signal.

Looking up, Love saw the signal and waved back. He rode off, then dismounted near the fuse bundle. He walked closer to the bundle, drew his pistol, and fired.

The shot ignited the bundle. The fuse began to hiss like a fiery snake.

The trapped prisoners screamed in fear as the burning fuse sizzled toward the powder kegs. They knew the blast would bury them alive.

From his hiding place Zorro watched as Montero

oversaw the final loading of the gold. There were still a few buckets left.

"Hurry!" Montero cried anxiously. "The fuses are burning!"

Hastily two guards covered the bed of the wagon and mounted. Love and his soldiers started riding away. As the horses trotted up the steep trail, the last two guards happened to turn around.

There, running along a scaffold, was a masked figure. Zorro sprinted toward the burning fuse, cloak billowing like black wings.

The two soldiers aimed their rifles and fired.

Instantly Zorro leaped from a ladder into a nearby mine tunnel.

At the sound of gunshots, Love pulled up his horse.

"Wait here!" he shouted to his men. Then he wheeled his horse and galloped back to the mine.

As Love approached, the two rear guards who had fired were racing up the scaffold after Zorro. But the prisoners screaming inside the cages saw only the burning fuse.

With each moment the hissing flame snaked closer to their doom.

Zorro scurried higher, the two guards in pursuit. Love galloped into the area and saw what was happening. He jumped off his horse and cut the burning fuse with his sword.

The prisoners sagged in relief against the bars.

Love started to climb the scaffold toward the waiting gold wagon. "Secure the wagons!" he yelled to his guards. "Stay alert!"

At that instant Montero saw Zorro running toward the

huge paddle wheel that lifted the elevator. He drew his rifle and turned to his men.

"Zorro!" Montero screamed. "There he is! Kill him!"

Bullets whined and cracked all around Zorro as he grabbed a wheel paddle and was pulled upward. Below him soldiers were reaching for the wheel ladder. Just in time, Zorro snatched the ladder from their grasp.

Turning, Zorro jammed the ladder into the center of the great wheel. The wheel screeched to a halt, stopping the elevator in midair.

But he was surrounded. The two soldiers who first spotted him had come around and climbed onto the wheel platform from the other side. Guns drawn, the two guards hurried to the wheel.

When they got there Zorro had vanished.

They looked around frantically. There was no place he could hide.

Suddenly Zorro dropped upside down from the top of the wheel. He grabbed each guard by the seat of his pants and heaved them over the edge.

Other soldiers were scaling the platform. There was no way to stop them—and no way off the platform.

Except one—the tension cable.

Using his sword as a slide, Zorro flew swiftly down the cable wire to the scaffold below.

As soon as Zorro landed, two soldiers rushed at him, swinging their swords. Zorro met their charge with a slashing blade, driving them back.

Love raced up the scaffold to join the fight, but he was a bit late. Montero already had Zorro in his rifle sight. It would be his honor to kill the masked outlaw.

Smiling grimly, Montero squeezed the trigger.

Swakk! A steel sword knocked the rifle aside, and Montero's shot went wild. Stunned, Montero turned and saw the tip of a sword jabbing into his throat.

"De la Vega!" Montero gasped.

Diego circled, then abruptly lunged, knocking Montero down with the hilt of his sword. Montero rolled over.

A familiar figure stared down at him—Elena.

The sight of his daughter spurred Montero's fury. Sword drawn, he scrambled to his feet and attacked. Diego blocked each thrust, but Montero's murderous intensity wore him down. As Elena watched, Montero's slashing blade drove Diego back to the railing.

On the other side of the mine, Zorro was in trouble. Soldiers were pressing in from both sides. Even his brilliant skills with a sword couldn't hold them back.

One soldier charged, blade inches from Zorro's heart. Zorro dodged, picked the soldier off the ground, and threw him bodily at the others.

The next instant he raced across the platform and leaped onto a nearby water chute. A pack of guards scrambled up the chute after him.

Zorro hopped onto the water tower and pulled the chain, unleashing a torrent of water. The rushing water blasted the soldiers out of the chute.

Hanging on to the pull chain, Zorro swung down from the tower. As he hit the ground, he glimpsed a tall guard running at him. The guard carried an ax with a pointed handle.

Suddenly the guard flung the ax directly at Zorro. As the weapon spun closer, Zorro realized both ends were lethal.

Zorro dodged, and the ax stuck in a post. The guard was still coming toward him at full speed. Zorro ducked low and flipped the guard, impaling him on the pointed ax handle.

Glimpsing a flash of movement, Zorro whirled. Love's blade missed him by inches.

Zorro smiled. "One question, Captain Love."

"What is that?" Love grunted, hacking at Zorro wildly.

"Where would you like your remains displayed?"

Roaring with anger, Love attacked, his blade lashing like a steel whip.

Across the yard Elena watched horrified as the four men in her life battled to the death.

Her two fathers, Diego and Montero, were engaged in an intense duel. Below them Love's troops had returned and dismounted. They began climbing toward Zorro and Love.

Love slammed Zorro against a beam and stabbed. The blade missed Zorro's quick body, but Love swung again. Zorro rolled away, his black hat flying.

Springing to his feet, Zorro turned in time to block a vicious chop.

For an instant their swords locked.

Muscles tensed like steel wire, the two men stood eye to eye—until Zorro's sudden head butt staggered Love. He stumbled back, tumbling down a slope.

Love crashed to a stop against the smelting house. Zorro leaped and rolled down after him. But when he reached the house, Love had vanished.

Four soldiers raced at Zorro, firing their guns.

Zorro ducked inside the smelting house, pulling his dagger. He knew Love was inside somewhere.

Unseen behind a huge steam boiler, Love cranked a valve wheel.

A metallic crack alerted Zorro just in time. He saw the steel boiler expand, and he leaped.

Krakoom! The boiler exploded, spraying chunks of hot metal like cannonballs. Clouds of fiery steam billowed through the door as the explosion ripped away the wall.

The blast blew the advancing soldiers off the stairs. Flaming sections of the house fell on the scaffold and ramp, setting them on fire. A half step ahead of the flames, Love raced to safety.

Zorro wasn't so lucky. Surrounded by smoke and fire, he blindly dived through a wall of flame. He tumbled down the burning water chute, rolled, and dashed up a nearby ramp.

Unfortunately a group of guards had headed down the ramp. Zorro whirled. More soldiers behind him.

He was trapped.

Zorro glimpsed a large crate hanging above the ramp. Instantly he lunged, his blade slicing the thick rope.

The heavy crate crashed down onto the loose planks, catapulting two soldiers high in the air.

Like circus tumblers the two guards flew over Zorro's head and landed in an ore cart. Zorro gave the cart a mighty shove, sending it hurtling down at the advancing soldiers.

To avoid being crushed, the guards leaped off the scaffold. Zorro spun around, looking for Captain Love.

Ignoring the explosion and flames, Diego and Montero fought on, their swords snapping like steel fangs.

With blurred speed Diego chopped Montero's sword out of his hand and lunged.

Diego's blade dug into Montero's throat. It was over. Montero was helpless.

"Now I am free to kill you," Diego rasped.

"No!"

Elena rushed to Montero's side. "Please don't!"

Elena's pleading eyes made Diego pause. He couldn't kill Montero in front of her. Slowly he eased his sword away from Montero's sweaty throat.

Without warning, Montero grabbed Elena's pistol and jammed it against her head.

Elena gasped in disbelief. Diego stood frozen.

"Drop your sword," Montero ordered.

Diego didn't hesitate. He let his sword fall to the ground.

A gleam of understanding lit Elena's face.

"You fool," Montero scoffed. "I never would have hurt her."

Diego looked at Elena. "I never would have taken that chance," he said softly.

Suddenly Elena knew her true father. At the same moment, Montero aimed the pistol at Diego—and fired point-blank.

"No!" Elena lunged, forcing Montero's arm aside. It wasn't enough.

The bullet slammed into Diego's body, spinning him to the ground.

17

ELENA RUSHED AT MONTERO, BUT HE FLUNG HER BACK like a sack of sugar. She crashed in a heap against the railing, dazed.

Blood streaming, Diego seized his sword and stood up, eyes glazed with fury.

As Montero picked up his fallen blade, Diego charged. Like bloody stags with steel horns, they clashed and staggered back.

The raging flames crept across the wooden structures, and thick smoke began to choke the prisoners locked in the cages. The fire spread to discarded crates and stacks of log beams and began to feed on the network of wooden trestles that webbed the mines.

Still searching for Love, Zorro ran back to the paddle wheel that operated the hanging elevators.

As Zorro approached, Love crouched down, waiting to ambush him. When Zorro's boot hit the platform Love sprang, sword slashing.

His blade sliced air.

Zorro wasn't there.

Love blinked. A heavy thump jerked his head around. Zorro dropped behind him and knocked him to the platform. Love scrambled up, sword hacking wildly.

"This time, by God, I will end it," Love ranted.

Zorro smiled grimly, sword humming like a deadly hornet. "I don't think God listens to you."

Fifty feet above them, Diego was weakening. The gunshot wound was starting to slow him down. Unable to mount an attack, he used his skill to defend himself.

Elena's eyes fluttered open. She glanced around and saw Montero and Diego dueling. Then she looked down and saw the cages. The prisoners inside were being engulfed by the thick smoke. The entire rail trestle was on fire.

And the flames were creeping nearer the cages.

Diego saw as well.

"Go, Elena!" he yelled, holding Montero at bay. "Get them out!"

Elena hesitated, still dazed. Finally she pulled herself together and staggered down to the cages.

Across the scaffold Zorro had Love on the defensive. Love retreated slowly under Zorro's intense attack.

Zorro's swift sword cut an *M* into Love's cheek. Love instinctively clapped his hand to his face. When he glanced at his palm he saw the bloody *M.*

"Murieta!" Zorro announced.

Love's eyes narrowed in recognition.

"And Zorro," Alejandro grunted, slashing at his enemy. "Two men—one death!"

Part of the scaffold was burning, but the two enemies

fought on, dodging the flaming debris that rained down on them.

Elena managed to jump away from a blazing chunk as it crashed to the ground. But the flames reignited the main fuse.

Once again the fiery strand began snaking down to the powder kegs. If any one keg exploded, the entire mine would collapse.

Zorro and Love remained locked in combat at the far end of the scaffold. A wall of flame shot up behind them. There was nothing ahead but the jammed elevators dangling in midair.

Zorro spun and backhanded Love to the floor.

Desperately Love looked around. He saw the rope that held the planks in place. The rope was within reach.

Love glanced back at Zorro, then swung his sword down. The sharp blade chopped the rope, and the plank flipped back, hurling Zorro off into space.

For a moment Zorro hovered in midair, like a black eagle. But as he landed on one of the elevators, he dropped his sword.

Without hesitation Love leaped off the scaffold. He landed on the elevator facing Zorro and attacked. Slashing viciously, he swung the elevator closer.

Unarmed, Zorro blocked Love's sword with the thick elevator cable. But Love's sharp blade frayed the rope. A few more hacks would send the elevator crashing to the rocks below.

Above them, Montero had Diego cornered.

His flashing blade slapped Diego's sword from his hand. Weaponless and wounded, Diego backed up against the gold-laden wagon.

Montero swung and missed. But his wild slash cut

right through the wagon harness. Spooked by the flames and the violence, the horses bolted free and galloped away.

Exhausted, Diego scrambled onto the wagon to escape Montero's deadly sword.

Knowing Diego had no place to hide, Montero moved in for the kill.

Below them, dangling in midair, Love swung the elevator closer to his helpless enemy. Zorro couldn't jump, and he couldn't fight. Smiling, Love thrust his sword at Zorro's exposed heart.

With incredible quickness, Zorro kicked the sword from Love's hand. Snatching the sword out of the air, Zorro struck!

A look of surprise crossed Love's face. Eyes wide, he looked down at the bright red stain spreading over his uniform.

He tried to hold himself erect by hanging on to the ropes. Slowly he sagged onto the roof of the elevator, blood gushing from the gash in his chest.

At the top of the mine, Diego lay bleeding in the horseless wagon. His eyes were fixed on Montero as the former governor lifted his sword.

Before he could strike, Diego suddenly released the wagon's hand brake. As the wagon rolled backward, the severed harness straps tangled around Montero's legs.

Screaming, Montero was dragged toward the edge of the cliff. At the last moment Diego jumped to safety. The wagon teetered, then plunged over the edge, spilling gold ingots—and taking Montero down with it.

Still battling Love, Zorro glanced up and saw the wagon tumbling over the edge of the cliff. With his free hand Zorro grabbed the whip hanging from his belt.

Heavy gold ingots pounded the elevator. Love looked up and saw the wagon hurtling toward him.

Snacckk! Zorro's whip snagged a high beam.

Instantly, Zorro leaped, swinging away just as the wagon smashed into the elevators. The impact sent both elevators, and Love and Montero, crashing to the rocks below.

A falling ingot narrowly missed Elena as she raced toward the prisoners' cages. She paused to pick up two pistols from a pair of fallen guards.

When Elena reached the first cage she wasted no time. She blew off the lock, then ran to the next cage as the prisoners burst out.

Dangling above, Zorro spotted Elena. He also noticed that the fuse had burned down to where all four fuses were joined. The sizzling fuses were heading down four separate mine shafts.

Alarmed, Zorro began climbing down to help Elena. She had reached the second cage and blasted the lock. The prisoners charged out.

When Zorro hit the ground, the fuses were only a few yards from the powder kegs.

Exhausted, Elena staggered to the last cage. But she had fired both single-shot pistols. Frantically, she hit the lock with a pistol butt.

From nowhere a hammer swung down and cracked the lock open.

Dazed, Elena looked up and saw the mask.

"Alejandro," she said breathlessly.

Without answering, he pulled open the door. As the prisoners spilled out, the fuses hit the kegs.

The explosion swatted the earth like a giant fist.

Flaming thunder boomed from the tunnels as they collapsed. A series of blasts shattered the sky.

Then a blanket of dense black smoke covered the mine like dirty snow.

And suddenly it was silent.

For long minutes the thick quiet loomed over the billowing dust.

A faint scuffling cut through. Then a ghostly shape emerged from the smoke. It was Alejandro. He had Elena by the hand as he led her and the prisoners to the safety of higher ground.

When they reached the crest, Alejandro spotted Diego crumpled on the ground. Hurrying to his side, Alejandro realized Diego's bullet wound was fatal.

Elena knelt beside her father with a canteen of water. She cradled Diego's head and put the canteen to his mouth.

Diego drank deeply, then looked up at Alejandro. "Is it finished?"

Alejandro nodded. "Yes, Diego. It is finished."

"But not for Zorro," Diego reminded him intently. "There will be other days, other fights. It is both your curse and your destiny."

Alejandro gripped Diego's hand. "So be it."

Diego smiled, knowing the spirit of Zorro would be safe with Alejandro. He turned to his beloved daughter.

"My beautiful Elena," Diego said gently. "Just when I find you, I lose you again."

Elena smiled through her tears. "You will never lose me . . . Father."

Beaming, Diego touched her cheek. "All I ever wanted was to hear you say that word.

"You were right about your mother," he went on. "You're just like her—her eyes, her smile, her spirit. And I know there's one thing she would have wanted for you."

Diego took her hand and placed it on top of Alejandro's hand. Elena and Alejandro looked at each other.

Slowly, Diego's hand fell away.

Sobbing softly, Elena put her arms around her father's body. Alejandro knelt beside her, grief flooding his heart like cold rain.

General Santa Anna arrived prepared for battle.

His fully armed Imperial Guards were mounted on forty warhorses. Every part of their equipment, from saddles to swords, gleamed in the sunlight.

At the head of the squadron, riding a magnificent white stallion, was Santa Anna himself, the general who had taken California from the Spanish king.

The squadron rounded a narrow bend and pulled to a sudden stop. Coming toward them from the smoldering debris of the gold mine was a ragged army of walking skeletons.

There were hundreds of them. Starved, wounded, exhausted, they staggered forward like ghosts, many still dragging their chains.

Two figures emerged from the center of the straggling mob: Alejandro and Elena.

Alejandro motioned for Elena to stay back, then came forward to meet General Santa Anna.

As Alejandro approached, two of Santa Anna's guards lifted their rifles. The general rode forward and signaled them to lower their guns.

Then he glared at Alejandro. "Who are you?"

Alejandro glanced back at the crowd, then at Santa Anna. "We are your people, Presidente."

Santa Anna turned to his lieutenant. "Look at them—in chains." He scowled at Alejandro. "And the mine is destroyed."

"You know about the mine?"

Santa Anna showed him a map. "I was told by the man who gave me this map."

It was the map Alejandro had stolen from Montero.

Alejandro tried to look innocent.

"Where is Rafael Montero?" Santa Anna demanded.

"He's dead."

"Then he is fortunate to have died when he did."

Alejandro was glad Elena couldn't hear. He was also aware that Santa Anna was frustrated, angry, and suspicious. To pacify the general, Alejandro pointed at the smoking piles of rubble.

"The gold is still under there, if you can dig it out. After all," Alejandro reminded him with a smile, "it belongs to you."

He was right. Santa Anna seemed to feel better immediately. He turned to his lieutenant. "Post guards around the area. Tomorrow we will search the rubble."

Suddenly Santa Anna noticed something. A square of black fabric had slipped out of Alejandro's belt. Blown by the desert wind, the black square lifted like a small kite.

It was caught in midair by a young boy.

Laughing, the boy put the black cloth over his face. It was a mask.

Zorro's mask.

"One moment," Santa Anna murmured. "Who was it that killed Montero?"

Alejandro hesitated. "Zorro."

A few coarse voices nearby shouted in agreement. Then the voices began to build. "Zorro!" the freed prisoners cried. "Zorro! Zorro! *Zorro!*"

About the Author

FRANK LAURIA was born in Brooklyn, New York, and graduated from Manhattan College. He has traveled extensively and published eleven novels, including three best-sellers and the novelization *Alaska.* He has written articles, short stories, and reviews for various magazines and is a published poet and songwriter. Mr. Lauria has also been an advertising copywriter and book editor. He currently resides in San Francisco, where he teaches creative writing. A film project based on his Doctor Orient series is in development.